"Then perhap   *ne."*

His inability to   her
past the point of   about his feelings. "Perhaps I
shouldn't."

"I'd like to change your mind, Ruth." He looked at
her with sad brown eyes. "But I don't want you to
become my wife because you feel you have to. I'll
ride with you back to your farm, but I won't come to
see you again unless you ask. If you haven't sent a
message to me by Sunday, I'll call off the wedding."

Ruth turned her back to him. "Please just leave me
alone. I'll make it back by myself."

"If that's the way you want it." His black's hoofbeats made the only sound as he rode away.

She wrapped her arms around her horse's neck and
buried her face in his mane. "What have I done, Sunset? I'm so confused I don't know anything anymore."
A fresh torrent of tears dimmed her eyes as she hoisted
herself into the saddle. "I can't become the kind of
wife they expect. But in another month, I won't be a
teacher anymore. I have nothing left." Scarcely noticing where Sunset took her, she let weeping take over.
She rode and cried until exhausted. Should she write
Theo about what had happened? If she didn't write
back, she wouldn't have to endure the pain of breaking off their letters when he married. She didn't think
she could endure this afternoon's grief again.

JANELLE BURNHAM is from British Columbia, Canada and has been writing for over ten years. *Beckoning Streams* is Book Two of the "Stories of Peace" series from **Heartsong Presents.**

Books by Janelle Burnham

HEARTSONG PRESENTS

HP53—Midnight Music
HP100—River of Peace

Beckoning Streams

Janelle Burnham

Stories of Peace—Book Two

Heartsong Presents

To Colleen L. Reece
Thanks for your encouragement, suggestions, and friendship.

I love to hear from my readers! You may write to me at the following address:

Janelle Burnham
Author Relations
P.O. Box 719
Uhrichsville, OH 44683

ISBN 1-55748-662-X

Beckoning Streams

one

Flanked by two men she had known since childhood, Ruth McEvan choked back the urge to flee the schoolroom crowded with strangers. Nervously, she checked the waistband of her dark green knee-length skirt to make sure it hadn't folded over and that her green print blouse remained well tucked in. She hoped her red shoulder-length hair hadn't been too badly mussed by the ride into town in Mr. Pierce's buggy. Her knotted stomach told her this meeting couldn't possibly bring good news. To her best recollection, there had never been a gathering of all the teachers and trustees in the district before. Each school had been managed by its own trustees and taught by teachers selected by those trustees, a system that had worked well for Peace River area farm families since a handful of parents had opened the first school twenty years ago. The provincial Department of Education had provided few guidelines and even less financial help over the years, leaving each school relatively autonomous. A meeting such as this could only signal changes.

She accepted the chair indicated by her own school's superintendent, Lars Harper, and tried to ignore the tension threatening to turn her stomach inside out. During the past seven years, her little school had become her life. She'd been just fourteen when it had opened on a bit of land donated by her dad, built by five nearby families, and taught by a petite, gentle lady from the city, Ida Thomas. Ruth knew she hadn't been an easy student in the beginning. A river accident had claimed her mother and three of her brothers less than two years previously, leaving her confused, angry, and responsible for helping her devastated father care for a toddler and a first-grader. Miss Thomas' compassion had worked its way past Ruth's bitterness and helped her begin to accept the tragic changes life had thrust upon her. Friendship had gradually developed between the two.

Ruth's dad, Timothy McEvan, had also been drawn to the school teacher. Ruth had rejoiced to see twinkles return to his eyes as he had spent increasing amounts of time with Ida Thomas. At the end of Ida's first year of teaching, they had married. It seemed natural for Ruth and her brothers to call their dad's new wife "Mom." Her caring heart provided the tender mothering they needed. The boys had been young enough that they didn't feel any conflicting loyalties. Ruth envied them their lack of memories. Her own memories of their mother and her twin brother, Daniel, sometimes brought feelings that she was betraying them by loving her new mother. She still couldn't understand why God hadn't prevented the accident. As she'd done often in recent months, she pulled her thoughts away from the unsettling question.

A year after Timothy and Ida's marriage, Ruth had graduated from the country school. Ida had encouraged her to continue her education in the recently established high school classes in town. Two years later, Ida had left teaching to have her baby, and Ruth had been asked to take her place. The trustees' request had come as a shock since Ruth had had no formal teacher training. But they'd insisted they had confidence in her abilities, so she'd taken the job.

Her lack of education weighed heavily in her thoughts as a well-dressed, balding man at the front of the room called the meeting to order. "As near as I can tell, we have a representative from each of the schools in the area. Seems like schools have sprouted around here like quack grass." Several chuckled at the intended joke. Ruth wasn't sure she liked the comparison. "The situation is this, ladies and gentlemen. There are thirty-nine schools around the area, not counting Dawson Creek's high school. Some of our schools are well-funded while others are just getting by. A few of us have been talking amongst ourselves and consulting with the Department of Education and we've come up with a solution which we hope will put all schools on an even footing without over-taxing certain districts. The plan is to consolidate all our schools, which should make them easier to administrate, as well. Gustav Olafson will explain how this proposal will work."

A tall, sparse man moved to the blackboard. In a deep voice that carried well, he explained as he drew a map of the area south of the Peace River. "This," he explained, making an X near the center of the board, "represents Dawson Creek. Rolla is here." He placed a mark northwest of the first, and another to the southwest. "And this is Pouce Coupe. Basically, the South Peace River block will be divided into three sections. All the students in a given area will attend a single school until they're old enough for high school." Three lines illustrated his point. "As you can see, a town is located in each area, giving us a logical location for the schools. Since Dawson Creek already has the high school, that town will have two facilities."

"What about the teachers?" one man toward the back

wanted to know.

The bald man took over. "With so many students in each area, we'll certainly need more than one teacher for each school. Those with certification who have taught the longest will have first chance at those jobs."

Ruth tried to ignore the feeling of loss that hit her like a blizzard. Her school gave her worth and purpose. Without it, she'd be nothing more than a spinster stranded in her parents' home. Nevertheless, she couldn't crumble. Not here in public.

The other trustee from her school, Doug Pierce, lifted his hand for recognition. "Is this plan mandatory for everyone?"

She could have hugged him for asking, even though she knew the answer wouldn't change anything. It felt good to have someone else fighting for what had suddenly become so precious.

The bald man smiled benignly. "Of course not. However, the proposed four schools will be funded by district taxes. Independent schools will not be eligible for this funding, so parents would end up paying twice for their children's education if they tried to maintain an independent facility."

"When will the new plan go into effect?" Mr. Pierce pushed for more information.

"We hope to have facilities ready for the first week in September. We'll use existing buildings in Rolla, Pouce Coupe, and Dawson Creek, but they'll need additions and improvements. Several carpenters will be kept busy throughout the summer." His tone implied pride in providing employment.

"What about transportation?" someone else inquired.

"Many of the youngsters in our area will have a four or five mile drive to get to one of the new schools."

Ruth didn't bother trying to follow the answer. While some country schools might get a reprieve due to distance, hers was one of the closest to town. She had less than three more months of the job she cherished. Then, as a result of a single bureaucratic decision, she'd be tossed aside like vegetable peelings.

Doug Pierce didn't waste any time leaving the meeting. With a firm hand on her elbow, he guided her through the crowd out to his buggy. He didn't bother trying to make small talk as they drove home. His sympathetic silence reminded her of his son, Theodore.

She let her thoughts linger on the young man she hadn't seen since Christmas. In the months immediately following the McEvans' tragedy, Theo Pierce had proven himself the truest kind of friend. Though Ruth had tried to push him out of her life along with everyone else, he'd refused to leave. He didn't force his way into her confidence; he'd merely waited until she felt ready to talk. Doug Pierce had spent hours helping Timothy McEvan around the farm, and Theo often accompanied his dad. He'd sit at the table with his textbooks while Ruth cleaned, cooked, and mended for her father and brothers. If she started talking, he'd close his books and give her his undivided attention. If she didn't feel like talking, he studied silently. When he had left the Dawson Creek area for medical school in Edmonton five years ago, she felt like part of her went with him. He'd kept his promise to write to her regularly and always made time for a visit on his infrequent trips home. If only he were around tonight! She visualized his dark, gentle eyes that seemed able to read her heart before she'd found words to describe her feelings, his straight black hair, and tall skinniness. She gave herself a mental shake. Theo wasn't here, and wouldn't be for quite some time. She had to cope alone.

Mr. Pierce reined the horse to a stop in front of the McEvan farmhouse. Climbing out of the buggy, he reached up to assist her. Retaining his grasp on her arm, he seemed to struggle for words. "Miss McEvan, Ruth." Thick dusk obscured his face, but Ruth heard the compassion in his voice. "I'm really sorry for what happened tonight. If there were a way to avoid closing your school, we would have found it."

"I know." She tried to put a smile into her tone.

"You're not only an excellent teacher but a very special person. Cynthia and I think of you more as a daughter than a neighbor. If we can help you in any way, even just by listening, please let us know." He hugged her tightly. "You need to talk with your dad, so I won't linger. Just don't forget we love you."

Lamplight flickering in a window indicated Dad and Mom had waited up for her. She opened the front door uncertainly, not sure how to explain the evening's events. Her parents sat in their favorite places at the end of the table nearest the stove, holding hands. Mom's waist-length hair hung down her back the way Dad liked it, firelight from the stove giving the blond strands a ruddy glow similar to Dad's rumpled curls. Dad let Ruth hang her coat on the hook and remove her boots before asking, "How was the meeting?"

Ruth met his blue-eyed gaze directly. "My school is being closed." She fought to say the words without choking up.

Mom instantly jumped to her feet and reached toward Ruth. "My poor girl." Though several inches shorter, she pulled Ruth's head down onto her shoulder in a purely maternal gesture of comfort.

Her caring proved to be Ruth's undoing. The tears she had choked back for hours now poured out in a hot torrent. A strong arm wrapped around her back as she felt both herself and Mom enfolded in Dad's embrace. In their comfort the intensity of her feelings ebbed. Mom led her to the table. "Do you feel like talking about it?"

She didn't really, but they deserved an explanation. She outlined the proposed changes much as the bald man had done.

Dad's expression looked thunderous. "You mean we're being forbidden to keep our own school?"

His defense of her school felt so good, a shaky smile stretched her lips. "No. They say the goal of the plan is to keep taxes low and schools well-funded. If parents are willing to support an independent school in addition to paying taxes, no one will object."

His temper abated as quickly as it flashed. "I have to admit it makes sense." He shrugged. "Pierce and Lars Harper have been trying to get more funding from the Department of Education, and I'm sure other schools have been doing the same."

Mom patted Ruth's arm. "It still hurts, though, doesn't it?"

Ruth nodded, tears scalding her eyes again. "I feel so useless."

"Why is that, Ruthie?" Dad's work-roughened fingers stroked her hair.

"What am I going to do once school is over?"

He grinned mischievously. "Rest, plant a garden, read, make pies."

She couldn't see the humor. "In other words, sit around like an idiot. Where am I going to find another job?"

"Why do you need one?"

She looked for understanding in their eyes, but saw only compassion. "I can't be dependent on you forever!"

"Why not?" Dad looked almost pleased.

"Because I'm a grown woman, that's why." Ruth struggled to keep her voice low enough to avoid waking the children. "You have the younger ones to take care of. I should be helping, not adding to the burden."

"You're never a burden, sweetie. In fact, I'm honored to be able to take care of you. That's my role as your dad. If the school hadn't needed you, I wouldn't have wanted you to work in the first place."

Ruth shook her head, desperation making her voice shrill. "You don't understand."

Mom placed a hand on Dad's arm to stop his reply. "Perhaps not. But because you're hurting, we hurt, too. We only want to help if we can. Can you trust us for that much?"

With effort, Ruth reined in her emotions and nodded. She shouldn't expect anyone to understand what she couldn't explain. No words she could think of would adequately describe the ache filling her chest. She'd lost more than a school or a job. She'd lost her identity.

two

Ruth left for school the next morning before her brothers finished the chores. She needed to be alone and counted on the extra hour before class to subdue her still roiling emotions. If only the meeting had been scheduled for a Friday or Saturday evening, rather than a Thursday. Now she had to face her students before she'd had a chance to adjust to the news. The proposed changes that monopolized her thoughts probably wouldn't be common knowledge for another couple of days. Even then, she had no intention of discussing them in her classroom. It would be up to parents to inform and reassure their offspring. Besides, she doubted any of them would be nearly as distraught as she felt.

She paused for a moment on the step in front of the schoolhouse door to look around. Bright sunshine promised change in the snow-blanketed landscape. Spring had always been her favorite time of year as snow gave way to dark earth, sprouting vegetation, and new leaves. But today, sunshine didn't bring the familiar tingle inside. It only reminded her that the last day of school hovered only ten weeks away.

Opening the door, Ruth stepped into the familiar room. Desks sat in tidy rows facing a blackboard on the far wall. Her own desk occupied the center front of the room between the blackboard and her students' desks. Off to the left, a small stove radiated warmth from the fire Dad had built earlier in the morning, as he had every chilly day for seven years. She hung her coat and scarf on the highest peg beside the door. In forty-five minutes, the short wall from the door to the corner would be filled with winter wraps. She'd never been able to figure out how her fourteen students could fill two rows of ten pegs each and still squabble over who had stolen whose peg.

She hoped today would be a peaceful one; she didn't think she'd be able to cope with any petty disputes or recalcitrant youngsters. "Please, just cooperate," she whispered pleadingly to the empty desks.

The routine tasks of preparing for her day brought a feeling of order. She organized papers to be graded, found a passage of Scripture for everyone to read together, wiped the blackboard with a damp cloth, and wrote the daily arithmetic quiz in place. At least for today, she was still a teacher.

Doug and Cynthia Pierce's thirteen-year-old daughter, Sara, arrived first. "I wanted to get here early so I could give you this," she explained with a shy smile. As much as her brother, Theo, resembled their dad, she looked like her mother. She had the same silky-looking straight black hair and gentle blue eyes. Though Cynthia stood about the same average height as her husband, Sara looked far more petite. She held a wrapped package toward her teacher.

Ruth accepted the bundle. "What is it?"

"Just some cookies." Pink tinged the girl's cheeks. "Dad told us what happened at the meeting last night, and I wanted to let you know we still love you."

Her gentle affection brought tears to Ruth's eyes, though she blinked them away quickly. "You don't know how much you've helped me," she managed to say and let a hug communicate the rest of her feelings.

Sara seemed to understand. Her eyes lit with merry twinkles. "There's also a letter from Theo in there."

Ruth felt like sunshine had finally broken out from behind a cloud. "Just for that, you'll get top marks on your next essay."

Sara just grinned and scampered outside to join the Harper and Spencer girls, who were giggling together. Ruth wanted to rip the package open immediately. However, she'd enjoy Theo's letter more if she could read it privately and uninterrupted. She slid the box under the edge of her desk. Just knowing what was in it would add cheer to her entire day.

Despite her hopes for a tranquil day, spring sunshine had given everyone the fidgets. Papers rustled, pencils broke, and books dropped. Just an hour before lunch, indignant shrieks shattered the tense semi-silence. "Phillip McEvan, I hate you!" Little blond Julie Harper glared at the innocent-looking redhead behind her.

Ruth looked up from guiding Audrey Spencer through a word list in time to see Julie slap Phillip with all the force of her ten-year-old indignation. "Miss Harper?" Ida had always said treating students like adults often brought out their best behavior.

"He pulled my braid, Miss McEvan, just when I had my penmanship page almost finished. Now it's totally ruined and I hate him." The girl dissolved into tears.

"Mr. McEvan?" Ruth looked to her young brother for an explanation.

"I was just teasing!" Phillip's blue eyes, so much like

their father's, filled with reproach. Rather than having a typically redheaded temper, thirteen-year-old Phillip approached life as though it were an adventure, everyone a friend. His casual approach to responsibility and good behavior gave his parents and his older sister many moments of despair. Ruth knew from experience the futility of trying to discuss the matter with him. His logic perceived the problem to be Julie's for overreacting. Similar situations in the past had taught her to give his seemingly boundless energy the outlet it required.

"I think you need to go outside and chop some kindling for the stove, Mr. McEvan. Julie, let's look at your page and see what can be done to fix it." A few rubs with an eraser eliminated the errant marks. As usual, the problem hadn't been nearly as severe as Julie's outburst had indicated. Her Norwegian family's emphasis on neatness gave the child more reasons than most for emotional displays. Anything that threatened the tidiness of her little world brought on tears or temper.

She'll learn soon enough how untidy life can be, Ruth commented to herself with a twist of bitterness, which she quickly squelched. Best to concentrate on the matter at hand, improving the six-year-old's reading skills.

An exhausting four-and-a-half hours later, she waved the last of her students off toward home, then snatched the box from beneath her desk. Lying on top of delicious-smelling oatmeal cookies lay an envelope marked in familiar handwriting. *Please give this to Ruth McEvan*, it said. With the cookies in one hand and the letter in the other, she settled herself in the sunbeam streaming through the open doorway.

My dear friend, the letter began.

*I take a few moments during this endless
night on duty to let you know I've been
thinking of you. I confess to envy as I consider spring coming to the Peace River
country. Every year I've been away, I've
intensely missed our tramps in the bush
hunting pussywillows and other signs of
spring. If you get a moment, would you take
some pussy willows to my mom for me? Is
the creek high enough to cover the beaver
dam? Remember the year it got so high you
couldn't even tell the dam was there? That's
kind of the way I feel around here. There's so
much to be done, I sometimes wonder if it's
really me taking temperatures, bandaging
wounds, and listening to heartbeats. But I'm
not unhappy or complaining. This is excellent training for whatever God wants me to
do next. As Mrs. Barry's favorite Scripture
verse says, 'The steps of a good man are
ordered by the Lord.'*

*Your last letter was wonderful. I love
hearing what all your students are doing. I
know you're teaching them well. While I
enjoy reading about the happy things in your
life, I hope you'll never hesitate to let me
know if things aren't going so well. Though I
can't be there in person for you, please
remember I'm no less your friend now than
I've been in the past.*

*Oops. I hear one of the nurses calling, so
I'll have to close for now. I'm praying for
you.*

Your pal,

Theo.

Ruth let the pages drop into her lap. The words brought
comfort even while they made her miss him even more.
He'd understand her feelings, maybe even help her make
sense of them. Right now she wouldn't even be able to find
the words to write to Theo. If God were so determined to
let this happen to her, why hadn't He made sure her best
friend were around to help her cope? The sour thought
startled her. When had it become so easy to blame God for
everything?

She stuffed the letter into her satchel, made sure the damp-
ers in the stove were closed, shut the schoolhouse door
firmly, and took a thin trail through the bush toward home.
Having worn this trail as a student in an effort to avoid her
brothers on their daily treks to and from school, she usually enjoyed its solitude in her transition from teacher to
sister and daughter. Today the pleasure had vanished. In
its place she felt anger, betrayal, abandonment, even confusion. Her trail joined the lane to their house just before
the farmyard. Dad was working with a spirited young horse
in the corrals beside the barn to her left. He waved and
smiled in greeting, the fabric of his shirt stretching tightly
across his muscled chest. It felt good to see him so happy.
In the two years immediately following her mother's death,
he had lost so much weight his clothes had hung on him
like a stick scarecrow's garb. Grief had stooped him to

almost normal height. Several months of Ida's love and cooking had finally straightened him to the broad, smiling giant of her childhood.

"How was school?" he called, letting the horse roam the corral while he bent over to lean his elbows on the rails. His rusty hair, which he'd passed on to Ruth and her brothers, lay in rumpled disarray from his efforts to control the skittish horse.

She quickened her steps to join him. They didn't often get time to visit, just the two of them. "Tiring."

"I didn't expect the day to be easy. I hope Phillip didn't make things more difficult."

His perception took her by surprise. "Actually, they were all on the edge of wild today. Spring sunshine does that."

"Phillip?" he insisted.

"He pulled Julie's braid this morning, though according to him the resulting war was her fault for slapping him."

Timothy chuckled. "That sounds like Phillip. What then?"

"I sent him outside to chop kindling. He came back with dirt streaks all over his pants. I didn't bother to ask what he'd been doing. After that, a muddy leaf just 'accidentally' landed on Julie's desk. He knows she's fanatically neat, so he delights in seeing how many ways he can find to make her mad."

"From what you and your mother have told me, it doesn't take much." His blue eyes twinkled.

She scowled at him. "Now you look like Phillip. Maybe I ought to get Mom to take the switch after you when he misbehaves."

He shrugged, now looking innocent. "Why me? I'm just his dad." Pushing back from the log rails, he straightened and reached for the reins he'd been using. "I'd better get back to work. I want to have Star ready to help me with planting. If the snow keeps melting like it has so far, I could be out in the fields by the end of next week."

Ruth continued leaning on the corral, watching Star. As far back as she could remember, she had loved horses. They had a grace she didn't see in any other animal, and all she'd met so far seemed genuinely affectionate. Star lunged at the end of the reins, not yet ready to accept Dad's direction. He hung on patiently until the animal settled.

Wearily, she turned toward the house. Once a simple two-bedroom cabin, it now boasted additions front and back. The front one had been built the summer after Dad and Mom's wedding and contained a porch and two bedrooms, one for Ruth and one for the boys. The back one had followed the birth of Beth, who was now close to two. It contained another two small bedrooms used by Beth and three-year-old Timmy. Ruth had offered to share her room when Beth grew old enough to be moved out of what was now called "the baby room," a cubicle near Mom and Dad's room that Ruth and the boys had shared until their rooms had been built.

"Thanks for the offer," Mom had said, "but you're an adult now and need your own space. The pigs sold well last fall, so we can afford it."

This afternoon, Ruth blessed Mom's wisdom. It felt heavenly to shut the rest of the world out for a little while. A stack of arithmetic tests and English compositions overflowed accusingly from her satchel, but she ignored them. She lay back on her bed, staring at the ceiling, finally letting feelings come to the surface. What if she ended up an old maid, living with her parents even after her hair had turned gray? That seemed to be all the future held for her. Guilt added to her gloom. Sure, Dad had said he'd consider it an honor to continue to support her, but had he considered the length of time he'd probably have to do it? She felt as if she stood at the edge of an endless progression of bleak years without purpose, fulfillment, or even identity.

Another alternative came to mind. She fished under her bed for the box in which she stored letters she wanted to keep. Most of them bore Theo's handwriting. Near the bottom lay one with perfectly scripted words, still holding a delicate scent. Ruth's earliest memory of Grandmother Carrington was seeing the stately, well-dressed lady descending the steps of Dawson Creek's first passenger train, her expression looking like she'd just stepped into a nightmare. Without even greeting her son-in-law or grandchildren, she'd announced she'd come to "take poor Janet's only remaining children back to civilization where they can be raised properly." Ruth had been sure her dad would give in until she saw the look on Ida's face. Though no formal courtship had yet developed between Ida and Timothy, the schoolteacher had looked ready to give her blood to keep the McEvan children in Dawson Creek. She'd even ridden out to the McEvan farm alone in an uncharacteristic breach of etiquette. Ruth remembered her kneeling in the snow to reassure Phillip as they'd passed her on their way to school. They'd never found out what she'd said to their dad, but Grandmother had returned to Toronto alone. Nevertheless, she'd written to Ruth at least twice a year, offering every enticement she could present to persuade her granddaughter to come east. Her most recent letter had arrived last week.

> *My dear granddaughter,"* it said.
> *I trust this letter will reach you in time for your twenty-second birthday. However, since your father insists that you live far beyond the reach of civilization, I won't be surprised if it is late. Please know I wish you the happiest of days.*
> *Since I have received no notice of your impending marriage, I have to assume your father has been as remiss in this area as in all others relating to your growth into a young lady. Should you decide to accept my long-standing offer to come live with me, I can assure you there will be no lack of young men seeking your hand. I'm sure I could arrange a marriage for you with one of our city's wealthiest families.*
> *If you prefer to further your education for a couple of years first, I could arrange entrance for you into one of our best schools, despite your age.*
> *I love you, dear, and truly wish to see you as happy as you can be.*
> *Your loving grandmother.*

Ruth stared at the fine paper, for the first time seeing beyond Grandmother's continuing disapproval of Dad. Maybe she should go east. At least she could further her education. She couldn't imagine living in the city forever, but maybe she could tolerate a year or two. Yet the thought twisted her heart. She'd miss seeing young Timmy and Beth grow up, being part of life on the farm she loved, watching her brothers become young men. Which would be worse, alienation from everything she knew and loved, or remaining helplessly useless in a familiar environment?

The impossible choice brought a wordless exclamation of frustration to her lips. Why did everything have to be so complicated? She flung the box back under her bed, then yanked a work dress over her head in place of her teaching clothes. Thinking wasn't getting her anywhere. She might as well make herself useful in the kitchen.

Mom sat at the table peeling apples. "Other than dealing with your brother, how did your day go?" Her understanding smile mellowed Ruth's mood.

"Not too bad. How did you hear about Phillip already?"

"I asked him about his day when he got home. He told me you'd sent him outside twice today."

"Spring has them all wound up," Ruth observed, hoping her tone wouldn't betray her tension. "Would you like me to make biscuits?"

"That would be perfect with the stew I have in the oven." Mom wiped the back of her hand across her forehead. A few blond locks straggled wearily around her face, having come loose from the graceful twist at the back of her head. "I'd planned to get this pie done earlier in the day, but I haven't had much energy. It's been all I could do to keep up with the little ones." Her usually vivid green eyes appeared faded.

Concern stabbed at Ruth. "Are you feeling all right?"

"Pretty good, all things considering." Whatever she had been planning to say was interrupted by a small, howling red-haired boy. "What is it, Timmy? Stop crying so Mommy can understand what you're saying."

Between sobs, the three-year-old managed to talk. "I just wanted to play with Gweggy's twuck, but he hitted me!"

"Let's ask Greggy about this, okay?" Mom scooped Timmy into her arms, and headed purposefully toward the bedroom.

Ruth heard scraps of the conversation, but didn't pay much attention. Altercations like this were common. Timmy tried valiantly to keep up with his older brothers, but they didn't want to be bothered with a toddler. Greg had been the baby of the family until Timmy had been born and then Beth just a year later. Though proud of the babies, neither of the older boys had much patience with the curious little ones who managed to investigate everything in the house. She formed one last biscuit from the leftover dough and set the full pan over the warming oven, ready to be baked as soon as the stew pot came out. In only a few more minutes, she had the pastry mixed, rolled out, and folded into two pie plates. After peeling and chopping the apples Mom had started to prepare, she mixed them with cinnamon and a touch of sugar and filled both pies, which she covered with another layer of pastry. The stew could simmer on the back of the stove while the biscuits and pies baked.

Mom returned just as Ruth shut the oven door. "Thanks, Ruth. I didn't intend for you to have to cook supper after a full day at school." She sank wearily into the rocking chair in the corner, Timmy snuggled against her shoulder.

"I used to have to do this all the time," Ruth reminded

her, "and I didn't have stew waiting, either."

"I've often wondered how you kept up with your studies so well with all you had to handle here at home."

"I guess a person just does what has to be done." Ruth shrugged.

"Scripture does say God never gives us more than we can bear," Mom replied. His feelings soothed, Timmy wiggled off her lap, though Beth quickly took his place. Almost from birth, she'd been a cuddly baby and still never lost a chance for a hug or a snuggle.

Ruth silently set bowls around the table. There it was again—the reminder that the all-powerful God she'd been taught to love had betrayed her. Sure, she'd survived, but His lack of action that day at the river still felt like a burden heavier than she could carry. He didn't seem prepared to bestir Himself to save her school, either. When she needed Him most, He became remote, hidden behind lofty-sounding Scripture verses. The anger felt so intense, she glanced over to see if Mom had noticed, but the two in the rocking chair were almost asleep.

Dad came inside just as she lifted the biscuits from the oven. "Smells heavenly in here." He breathed in deeply, then leaned over to kiss his wife.

She stirred, her eyes fluttering open. They brightened to their normal color as she saw the big, red-haired man leaning over her. "Hi, honey."

Dad studied her intently. "How're you feeling?"

"Pretty good after a short snooze." Mom pulled his head down for a long kiss.

A silly grin played around his lips. "Hmmm. That's quite a welcome." Concern replaced the grin. "I don't like to see you so tired, though."

Her eyes glowed with the special light meant only for him. "You don't need to start worrying just yet."

"Can't help it," Dad muttered, turning toward the wash basin.

The undercurrent more than words or actions seemed familiar to Ruth. Dad's fretting. Mom's weariness. No explanation presented itself. She glanced at Mom stroking Beth's blond curls with a look of supreme happiness. How would it feel to be so cherished by a husband, so fulfilled as a mother?

Dad's arrival brought the three boys barrelling from the bedroom, chattering excitedly. Dad tossed Timmy into the air, rumpled Greg's hair, and thumped Phillip's shoulder. "And how are my two scholars? Did you make Ruth's day a good one?" He winked at his daughter.

All three boys tried to talk at once while Dad herded them toward the basin to wash their hands for supper. Ruth's doldrums lifted as the family settled around the table. Phillip and Greg bantered back and forth as usual, keeping the adults laughing. Dad praised the biscuits. Mom complimented the pie filling. Before Timmy left the kitchen, he held his arms up to Ruth for a quick hug and Beth copied him. Their simple affection left Ruth with a smile as she washed dishes. Nothing in her life had been predictable since that day at the river. Things were changing again, but she still had a family who needed her. Their love would have to be enough for now.

three

"Are you ready, Ruth?" Mom called from just outside the closed bedroom door.

Ruth made no effort to move off the bed where she had lain for the last couple of hours. Though exhausted from two nights with little sleep, her mind hadn't slowed down enough to let her rest. Whatever she'd been scheduled to do, she didn't feel up to it.

"Ruth?" Mom pushed the door open gently. "What's the matter? We're supposed to be at Harpers' bonfire party in thirty minutes."

"I think I'll just stay home." Ruth kept her gaze focused on the ceiling.

"It might be good for you to go." Mom lowered herself gently onto the edge of the bed. "I know you feel like being alone, but you'll just lay here and think. An evening out in the fresh air could be just what you need to help you sleep tonight."

Ruth doubted Mom's logic, but knew better than to argue. She pushed herself into a sitting position. "Maybe so. It will just take me a minute to change." A denim skirt that reached several inches past her knees and a navy-and-white striped blouse made a comfortable outfit. The long, green wool shawl Mom had given her for Christmas several years ago would keep off the evening's chill. Since spring thaw conditions required rubber boots, she pulled on a pair of thick navy socks. A brush brought some semblance of order to her wavy hair.

The rest of the family had already piled into the wagon when Mom and Ruth came out of the house. Dad helped Ruth onto the plank, bench-like seat near the back of the wagon and Mom onto the front seat with him. Phillip and Greg sat with Ruth while Timmy and Beth played in some straw between the two planks. A cloudless sky indicated perfect weather for an evening outdoor party. Dusk wouldn't intrude until around nine o'clock. Only dirty patches of unmelted snow and a chilly breeze provided reminders that spring had only just begun.

Ruth ignored Phillip and Greg's conversation about a tree fort they wanted to build. A feeling of isolation settled around her like a heavy wool blanket. *This is what the rest of your life will be like*, she told herself. *You might as well get used to it.*

A mere thirty-minute ride brought them to James and Ruby Harper's well-ordered farmyard. A two-story farmhouse stood off to the left of the driveway that continued toward a massive barn. Just a couple hundred yards behind the farmhouse, a small cabin peeked out from behind some trees. It had been James and Ruby's original home and was now occupied by their oldest son, Jim, and his wife, Norma. Across the driveway from the house, a large area had been cleared where a number of people already milled around a crackling blaze.

Jim came running from the barn to greet the newcomers. "Good evening, Mr. and Mrs. McEvan. If you'd like to join the others at the fire, I'll take care of your horses." He lifted his hat toward Mom and then Ruth.

"Thanks," Dad replied, handing Jim the reins. Jumping down from the wagon, he lifted Mom down then handed her the basket of cookies she'd brought. Phillip leaped over the side to go join a muddy soccer game near the barn. Greg waited until Dad had helped Ruth to the ground, then handed Beth and Timmy down. Despite her mood, his thoughtfulness made Ruth smile. At ten, he already resembled what she remembered of Daniel.

Mom's basket of cookies joined the array of baked goodies on a long table made of rough planks laid over sawhorses. Ruth followed her family to the logs arranged like benches around the fire. With all the people who had come, she found it easy to remain unnoticed, which was just how she wanted it. She didn't feel like socializing, though watching everyone else gave her something neutral to think about.

Her school superintendent stood talking with his brother near the fire. Lars Harper's slender frame appeared short and emaciated beside James' stocky, broad-shouldered height. Lars had straight blond hair, but James had only a fringe around his ears. James appeared to do most of the talking while Lars listened.

Both Harper farms had become large, successful enterprises. Lars and his grown son, Jed, raised some of the best horses in the country, while James and his son, Jim, were developing a dairy herd and increasing their pasture and cultivated acreage annually. The fuel for tonight's bonfire had come from their continual clearing efforts. Both Jed and Jim had been among Ruth's first classmates when the school had opened. They had only stayed a year, however, choosing the next fall to become full partners in their parents' farms.

Jim's younger brother, Justin, had graduated from the country school in its second year, though he hadn't followed Mrs. McEvan's encouragement to go on to high school. Instead, he'd found a job in Dawson Creek's telegraph office and moved into town soon after. To Ruth's surprise, he'd come to the party tonight. His matching pants and vest with a white shirt seemed rather dressy for the evening's activity, but that was Justin. Fancy clothes suited his long-legged, slender frame well. He kept his blond hair carefully slicked back at all times. In the five years he'd been working in town, he'd gradually assumed sophisticated mannerisms. Some people said he thought himself too good for farm folks. His work brought him into contact with exciting events in the world beyond Dawson Creek, and he loved to talk about them. He seemed to fancy himself a dispenser of superior knowledge, yet Ruth found his revelations fascinating. Sometimes he showed up at the McEvan farm to try to persuade her to accompany him to a town function. She usually declined. The thought of being alone with him made her inexplicably uncomfortable.

As usual, tonight he'd found an audience. His sister, Patricia, and her husband, Bruce, looked only slightly bored as he imparted his knowledge. Only a few months younger than Ruth, Patricia had married Bruce Henderson soon after finishing school. In four years, they'd developed a small farm three miles northwest of her parents' and increased their family with three children. Envy stabbed at Ruth. Why couldn't her own life have turned out as comfortably?

Her attention shifted to a matched pair of sorrel horses

pulling yet another wagon into the driveway. The breeze ruffled their light-colored manes against their golden coats. She wished she could pet the beautiful animals without drawing attention to herself. If she ever had enough money to buy her own horse, she'd find either a sorrel or a bay. The solid color with contrasting mane seemed to her the best accent for a horse's grace and strength.

As the wagon came to a stop, she finally noticed its occupants, the Spencer clan. Mom hurried over to greet Mrs. Spencer, one of her closest friends, with a hug while Mr. Spencer relinquished his reins to Jim. Meanwhile, five of their six children dashed off toward the soccer game. Only the eldest, young Lionel, stood still, as if looking for someone. Ruth glanced at Sara Pierce in time to see her eyes light up and a flush spread across her cheeks. Young Lionel tried to appear casual as he made his way over to where Sara and her mother sat.

With her attention on the two youngsters, Ruth didn't notice the approach of a plump woman until it was too late to move. Lars Harper's wife, Kate, was the last person she wanted to visit with. "So, I hear you're out of a job come June," the lady announced as she approached. "That's too bad, but then maybe it will give you a chance to get married and settle down." She perched on the edge of the log beside Ruth. "It won't be long before you're past the marrying age. You know, I always thought you and Theodore Pierce would make a match of it. He must have decided he wanted to be a doctor more. Funny what men think sometimes, isn't it? I'm sure he'll be looking for a nurse, now. I'll have to remember to ask Cynthia if she's heard anything."

Ruth wished Mom or Mrs. Spencer were there to stop Mrs. Harper's flow of words. They were the only two she knew who could do so. Besides, she needed desperately to hear Mom's oft-repeated explanation. "Mrs. Harper doesn't mean any harm. She's just so interested in people, she doesn't think before she speaks." Tonight of all nights Ruth didn't feel up to being understanding.

The monologue continued. "Did you see my Nettie here with her husband? He's just as besotted with her as the day they were married. Now that she's in the family way, he treats her like fine china. You should come over and meet him. I haven't heard him mention having an unattached older brother, but we could ask."

Ruth suppressed a cringe, wondering how to decline gracefully. With a feeling of intense relief, she saw Mrs. Spencer beckoning. "Is Mrs. Spencer looking at you or at me?"

"Probably me." Mrs. Harper chuckled infectiously. "It's been nice visiting with you."

Ruth searched through the crowd for Nettie Harper, or Williams, as her name had become. She remembered the rambunctious know-it-all from her days as a student. Nettie had mellowed a bit by the time Ruth took over as teacher, but there had been a few tense days just the same.

"Would you like a cup of juice?" a quiet male voice inquired from behind.

Ruth turned to see Jed Harper extending a full mug. From under one arm his hat protruded, its imprint still showing on his curly light brown hair. Lines around his gray eyes already testified to hours spent in the outdoors squinting against the sun. In overalls and a faded flannel shirt, he looked every inch a typical Peace River farmer. Almost as soft-spoken as his dad, he'd never said more than "hello" to her. Curiosity about his motive kept her from irritation at being disturbed again. She tried for a friendly but neutral tone as she stood to take the cup. "Thank you for thinking of me."

"No trouble. I just noticed you weren't watching the soccer game and thought you might like some refreshment."

"I get to watch soccer every day at recess. Do you not like soccer?" She smiled to see if he would respond in kind.

His lips twitched slightly in what appeared to be his version of a smile. "After a full day following two horses and a plow, it's a treat to sit still."

"I imagine your mares will be foaling soon."

A sparkle of interest replaced shy hesitation in his eyes. "Hopefully we'll get a full dozen this year."

"Are they all thoroughbreds?"

"No." He set his wide-brimmed hat on the log and stuffed the hand that had been holding his hat into his pocket. Tapping one foot nervously beside his hat, he continued. "Thoroughbreds make nice riding horses, but they're no good for heavy farm work. We only breed a couple each year. The rest are either draft horses or mixed breeds." He stopped as though suddenly realizing he'd said more than a dozen words. Red tinged his ears.

She tried to think of a reassuring reply. "I like horses."

He nodded. "So do I." His well of conversation seemed to have dried up completely. They stood in uneasy silence for a few moments before he reached for his hat. "I'll be going now."

Ruth settled back onto the log. If he were a polished

charmer like his cousin, Justin, she would have thought he brought the juice as an excuse to talk with her. Talking obviously made him uncomfortable, so why had he come?

"You look thoughtful. I hope they're pleasant thoughts." A short, comfortably rounded woman with white hair sat down beside Ruth as if she'd been invited.

"Grandma Lucy!" Ruth impulsively gave her a hug. "I didn't know you were here."

"I came with Lionel and Nina. They refuse to let me miss out on anything around here." A wide smile made her plump cheeks even fuller.

"I must have been so busy watching your grandson I didn't notice you." Ruth felt her gloom vanishing. Grandma Lucy actually had no biological relationship with the McEvans. She'd offered a room in her boarding house for Ida Thomas when the teacher had been hired seven years ago. She and Ida became close friends as the younger woman adjusted to a new place and to living without her mother who'd died just six months before Ida came to Peace River. Lucy Barry had seen the attraction between Ida and Timothy even before they recognized their own feelings. On Ida and Timothy's wedding day, Lucy had insisted on taking Ruth, Phillip, and Greg for a week so the newlyweds could have time to themselves. That was the week Ruth and her brothers had started calling Mrs. Barry "Grandma Lucy." All of the children's natural grandparents still lived in Ontario, where the McEvan family had lived before coming to homestead in the Peace River area, so they cherished their adopted grandmother.

Grandma Lucy's eyes sparkled with interest. "You mean the one who has eyes only for young Sara Pierce?"

Ruth giggled. "Yes, that's the one. He tried to be so subtle, but their faces gave it away."

"He reminds me of his father at that age. My Lionel looked just the same the first time he laid eyes on Nina. Eighteen years later, they're still sweethearts. Have you heard from Sara's older brother lately? He's almost finished with medical school, isn't he?" Grandma Lucy had a way of asking personal questions in a way that conveyed loving interest rather than just curiosity.

"Actually, he finished school a year ago, but he has to do an internship at a city hospital before they'll let him work on his own."

"Any idea when he's coming home? I know Doug and Cynthia miss him terribly."

"He hasn't said yet. I'm sure if he'd made any plans, Sara would have announced it the next day at school."

"Do you think he'll stay in the city?" Grandma asked with an oddly intent look.

Ruth shrugged. "He hasn't mentioned anything like that. I know his mother keeps hoping he'll come back here to set up his practice."

"And what do you hope?"

"I haven't thought much about it," Ruth answered truthfully. "He's still my best friend, so it would be nice to have him home."

Grandma patted Ruth's hand. "Have you written to him yet about your school closing?"

She shook her head. "I don't know what to say."

"It hurts pretty badly, doesn't it?"

Tears stung her eyes, but she blinked them back. "I haven't thought of much else since the meeting Thursday night."

"I've been praying for you." The simple words conveyed infinite empathy and concern. "I hope you won't hesitate to come for a visit if you need to talk."

"Thanks." Ruth dredged up a genuine smile.

Grandma Lucy didn't say any more. Ruth couldn't help but feel the contrast between this silence and that which had fallen between her and Jed. The other had been isolating. This was the comfort of being both understood and loved.

four

Life is strange, Ruth mused, watching the children at recess. Only a month ago, she'd been content in her role as school teacher, with rarely a thought for the lack of romance in her life. Now it seemed she saw couples wherever she looked.

At the edge of the schoolyard, two figures wandered apart from the rest. Sara Pierce and young Lionel. *At least they never try to sneak out of sight*, she thought with relief. Both responsible youngsters alone, they had earned even greater trust from their parents in their conduct together. Though they often pulled apart from a group for private discussions, they always stayed in full view of adults. Ruth had yet to see them try to so much as hold hands. If she had to have lovebirds in her classroom, she thanked the Lord they were these two.

The rest of the children were playing a screeching game of "Kick the Can." She reflected on how much her students had grown during her three years as their teacher. She'd started with most of them at the middle level. Young Lionel Spencer would start high school next year and his brother, David, would follow him a year later. Their sister, Clara, had another two years before deciding whether or not to go beyond grade eight. It had been difficult to persuade June Harper to stay in school this year, so she probably wouldn't be back after the summer. Mom's first class of readers, all five now in their teen years, were now in grade seven. Her middle students, Julie Harper, Greg McEvan, and Tabby Spencer, would be in the new school for several years to come, as would Ruth's lone new reader, Audrey Spencer.

Ruth sighed. No matter which way she looked at the possible future, this school would be no more. It probably would have closed soon, anyway, since there wouldn't have been any new readers next year. "Consolidation," as it had been called, was obviously the best idea. But its effect on her life remained too painful to contemplate just now. Time to call her students in. She rang the bell. As usual, her three thirteen-year-old boys, Tommy Spencer, Teddy Harper, and Phillip, were the last to make it inside. She opened her mouth to reprimand them when Sara tugged on her sleeve. "Miss McEvan, look at what Lionel and I found."

A tiny nest snuggled in Sara's hand. A couple of spotted eggs lay inside. Ruth gasped at the delicate beauty of the woven twigs. "Where did you find this?"

"Over by that stump." Sara pointed. "There were feathers scattered all around, so Lionel said it looked like a fox or something had killed the mother."

Ruth grinned at the young man hovering nearby. "If you say that's what happened, I'll take your word for it." Young Lionel had already gained a reputation for being an exceptional tracker and reader of the bush country surrounding them. "I'll get everyone settled and you can tell us about your discovery." She turned toward her desk, then stopped. Her three "troublemakers" stood in front of it, holding a crudely lettered sign which read, "Happy Birthday, Miss McEvan!" From where she stood, she could read where each of her thirteen students had signed the banner and written a personal message. "I don't know what to say. This is a wonderful surprise." She blinked back tears that seemed to flow too easily these days.

"That's not all." Clara and Tabby scurried out the door and returned carrying a saddle blanket woven in tones of blue. "Greg and Phillip said you like blue, so we pooled our money to buy this for you."

Ruth looked at her students in amazement. Few of them ever had spending money, so parents must have contributed heavily. Regardless, her students had gone to incredible effort to provide her with a memorable birthday gift. She took the blanket from the girls to feel its roughness against her cheek. If only she had a horse to put it on. *Someday.* "I thank each of you. I can guess how you found out it was my birthday," she pretended to glare at her brothers, "and it means a lot to me that you'd work so hard to make it special."

"Can we go home early then?" irrepressible Phillip asked.

"No. We still have arithmetic quizzes to take." But by midafternoon, she relented. Early dismissal for one day wouldn't hurt any of them. Her brothers were the first out the door, but she called them back. "Would you take this home for me, please, and let Mom know I'll be there in a while?"

"Sure," Phillip answered amiably, reaching for the blanket, but Ruth pulled it back.

"Can you keep it out of puddles, off the ground, and away from blanket-eating trees?"

"Of course." The familiar reproach showed in Phillip's eyes.

"I'll take care of it," Greg offered. "We won't do anything else until we've put it in the house."

Ruth smiled her thanks. She knew Greg would keep his word. Phillip didn't mean to be irresponsible; he just got distracted easily. Leaving the schoolhouse door open, she sat on the step to grade quizzes. The warm sunshine felt soothing. Two of Julie's precisely written answers were incorrect. Tomorrow Ruth would have to explain yet again that incorrect answers didn't mean failure. On the other hand, Phillip wouldn't be at all disturbed by the fact his paper contained more wrong answers than right ones. Would their teacher next year make allowances for their different personalities? *Of course,* she reassured herself. The person wouldn't have been hired unless he or she was a good teacher. But Ruth's concern lingered. She'd miss seeing Tommy's eyes light up when he figured out how to do six-digit multiplication or Sara's dreamy expression while she worked on an English composition. All at once, she knew how to write to Theo so he would understand.

She retrieved a couple of sheets of clean writing paper from her drawer. Using a textbook as a lap desk, she began.

> *Dear Theo,*
>
> *Thanks again for taking time to write to me. The reminders of your steadfast friendship were exactly what I needed.*
>
> *Your letter arrived at the right time. Just the day before, I had attended a meeting of all the school trustees in this area. To put it succinctly, all of the one-room schools in the south Peace River district are being consolidated into four centrally located schools. While some teachers will be reassigned,*

others of us won't be.

*My life has been so centered around this
school, I feel like its closing is almost the
end of me. As I graded papers this afternoon,
I thought of what each student's personality
contributes to my day and how much I'll
miss them. It feels like when Daniel drowned,
like part of me has been cut off.*

*Meanwhile, everyone around me seems to
have found the proper place. Starry-eyed
couples and new babies abound while I look
forward to spending the rest of my days
turning into an old maid in my parents'
house.*

*Have you had time to take any pretty
nurses to dinner? Somehow I can't imagine
you in city dress-up clothes.*

Ruth reread her last paragraph several times. Why had
she written it? If Theo wanted to tell her about his dates,
he would. To eliminate the question, though, she'd have to
re-write the whole page. Folding the paper into her satchel,
she decided to think about it later.

She took her time wandering between school and the farm.
In a few weeks, this trail would be a shady refuge, but this
afternoon buds had not yet begun to form on the dead-
looking branches around her. Sunlight streamed between
them uninhibited. After months of cold weather and gray
skies, she revelled in the bright warmth. For today, at least,
she had something to look forward to.

Mom had a way of turning birthdays into full-scale cel-
ebrations. Everyone but the birthday person participated

in choosing presents, though no one breathed a clue until after the specially prepared dinner. Ruth had chosen chicken pot pie for this year's birthday meal, with egg pudding and canned raspberries for dessert. Her mouth watered at the thought.

In the barnyard, Phillip and Greg leaned on the fence watching Dad work with Star. She noticed how well the horse responded to his direction. The boys flashed her mysterious-looking grins, but said nothing in greeting. The house had a feeling of mystery about it, too. This feeling of suspense enhanced the joy of a birthday, knowing something delightful would happen in a few hours but also knowing there was no choice but to wait. Mom refused Ruth's offer of help in the kitchen. "Go take a nap or something," she advised, pretending to be irritable. "I don't want you here under my feet."

Ruth felt uncomfortable not helping, but did as she was told. The sunshine she enjoyed so much made bright patches on her bed and floor. She stretched out and closed her eyes, but sleep eluded her. The last two sentences she'd written to Theo haunted her. It shouldn't matter what he did with his spare time, but Mrs. Harper's comments wouldn't leave her alone. Ruth thought she wanted whatever would make him happiest, so why her mental tumult? *It's not the marriage part that concerns me,* she told herself resolutely. *It's the thought of him living so far away.*

She retrieved the paper from her bag and added to the paragraph.

> *After writing that question, I wonder if perhaps I'm being too nosy. Feel free to tell me it's none of my business. Something Mrs.*

*Kate Harper said the other day just made me
curious.*

*I'm now at home in my bedroom, awaiting
my mother's call to supper. I wish you were
here to celebrate my birthday with us. Have
you ever considered how strange it is that
you and I are such friends? A lot of people
wouldn't believe a man and a woman could
be just best friends.*

*With spring in the air, I've been watching
an example of the other kind of rapport that
can exist between men and women, or boys
and girls in the cases I'm thinking of. Your
sister is one of them. As I'm sure you're well
aware, she and young Lionel Spencer are
quite taken with each other. She looks like
spring sunshine whenever he's around.*

*I've never felt that way about anyone. Of
course, when I was Sara's age, I was becom-
ing a bitter old woman already. Thanks to
you and Ida, I've been able to leave that
behind.*

*I still think a lot, though, about the love I
always saw in my dad's face when he looked
at my first mother. He simply shrivelled up
inside when she drowned. Then he met Ida,
and his heart shows in his eyes again. Isn't
that kind of devotion just too risky? I hope
no one ever feels so strongly about me. I
know I'd never be able to feel the same,
because I'd always be afraid of losing him.*

I can't believe I'm writing these thoughts.

*I've never told anyone else about them, but
then I've told you many things no one else
knows about. You're a better friend than I
ever could have asked for.*

*I just heard Mom holler outside for the
guys to come in for supper, so I'd better
close this. Thanks for always caring about
what bothers me.*

Everyone came to the table in dress clothes. Even little
Beth wore her Sunday dress. Mom had prepared sugared
carrots to go with the pot pie and had set out a dish of
dilled beans. Every time Ruth looked at Greg, he giggled
and ducked his head as if he were afraid she'd read the
secret in his eyes. Actually, everyone looked more excited
than usual. She knew better than to ask, so she concen-
trated on enjoying the tasty meal.

When everyone had eaten their fill, Mom cleared the
dishes away and replaced them with dessert. Ruth looked
around for the pile of packages that usually accompanied
this part of a birthday dinner. Dad caught her glance.
"We've decided to stretch out the suspense a little more."

"That's not nice," she protested.

"We just didn't want age to make you set in your ways,"
he teased.

Ruth had almost finished her second helping of pudding
and berries when Greg and Phillip bolted from the table.
After peering out the door, they beckoned to her. "Come
look, Ruthie."

Her parents' smiles stretched wider. "Go ahead," Dad
encouraged.

She left the table hesitantly, half afraid her brothers had
devised some kind of prank. Only an approaching visitor

met her gaze. Seated on his magnificent black stallion, Jed Harper rode down the lane at a trot with a sorrel gelding following on a lead rope. The sorrel's flaxen mane and tail rippled as he tossed his head and pranced sideways. Ruth longed to feel his gallop beneath her. Her gasp brought a chorus of "Happy Birthday's." She looked back at Dad. "A horse for my birthday?" she asked in disbelief.

He nodded. "From all of us."

The gift seemed too wonderful to be real. "So that's why the children at school thought I needed a saddle blanket. Pretty sneaky, you two." She grabbed both brothers in a rough embrace then bolted out to meet her new friend.

Jed relinquished the lead rope. "He's already broke to saddle."

The horse stopped prancing when Ruth stroked his nose. "You're such a pretty boy. I'd like to take you for a run, but I have a party first. We'll go tomorrow all by ourselves." She led him in several circuits of the farmyard, talking quietly to get him used to the sound of her voice.

Dad met her at the barn door. "Bring him in here and see how he likes it."

Ruth tugged gently on the rope, and the horse followed. Dad led the way to a stall with a thick layer of fresh hay. A brand new saddle sat on top of the gate. She looked at Dad with wide eyes. "You shouldn't have spent so much!"

He laughed. "This isn't from us." He pulled a piece of paper from underneath the saddle and handed it to her.

"*Happy Birthday, Ruth,*" the note read. "*We hope this saddle brings you as much joy as you've brought us. Love, Doug, Cynthia, Theo, and Sara Pierce.*"

Happy tears filled Ruth's eyes. "I've always admired Mr. Pierce's leather work. I can't believe he made this just for me."

"You're worth it. Let's turn your friend out into the corral and see if Jed would like to join us in a checkers tournament."

The McEvans had spent many happy hours over the checkerboard. During the winter or on special occasions, the entire family participated in tournaments that could last several hours. Tonight, Beth and Mom played against Timmy, who won. Jed then offered to have a game with the little boy, who won again and went to bed feeling like a genius. With the toddlers asleep, fun began in earnest.

Jed appeared to relax quickly. At first, his few words were directed mostly at Timothy. After awhile, he offered suggestions to help Greg beat Phillip, then moves that helped Greg beat Ruth. Around ten o'clock, he emerged the winner. "Sorry to win and run," he apologized to Mom, "but the stock will be hollering at five tomorrow morning."

"Come again whenever you have the time," Dad offered.

"Thank you, sir." Jed looked at Ruth. "Happy birthday."

"Thanks for bringing the horse over. He's the nicest birthday present I've ever received."

Jed's face turned pink. "Glad to do it."

Ruth lingered at the corral after Jed rode off. Her horse stood at the far side, his golden coat picking up the last glints of daylight. *Sunset.* The term seemed to fit, though some might think it too fanciful. She called him softly. "Sunset." He nickered back and she relished the sound of her very own horse. It seemed unbelievable how so many people had participated in making her day joyous. With such an outpouring of love, why did she still feel so empty inside?

five

The next day was Saturday, so Ruth made herself a picnic lunch and saddled Sunset. His excellent training showed in the way he stood quietly for the entire procedure. Dad held the corral gate as she rode out. "You'll stay on our land?" he questioned.

"Yes. I'm going to take him for a run on the road, then we'll come back and be mostly down by the creek."

He nodded, grinning at her eagerness to be gone. "Take care on the road, and don't get too far out. If you're not back by nightfall, we'll start at the creek."

"I want to be back by midafternoon so I'll still have time to go into town to visit Grandma." She waved in farewell and urged Sunset into a trot. Once on the road, she let him have his head. As his stride lengthened, she leaned lower over his neck. "Good fellow. Let me see what you can do." As if in response to her words, his muscles swelled, giving their utmost. His gait was smooth and even, just like a dream horse ought to be. They galloped past the schoolhouse and beyond what she still thought of as Theo's home, a mile and a half west of the school. She slowed Sunset to a trot, then turned him back. Passing Pierce's farm for the second time, she realized it had been some time since she'd visited Mrs. Pierce. She'd have to take Sunset over to show them how well their gift suited him. *Someday soon,* she promised herself. With her own horse to ride, distance would no longer curtail her activities. But today was hers alone. She directed Sunset down a trail leading to her favorite retreat near the creek.

As the bush thickened, she dismounted and led him carefully through the trail she'd worn over the years until they came to an open area on the creek bank. A large, flat rock lay in perfect position for losing one's self in watching the creek rush or amble by, depending on the season. Today, still swollen with spring run-off, the creek flowed swiftly along. Tying Sunset where he could eat his fill of new grass while she daydreamed, she relaxed on her natural bench with her chin propped in her hands and elbows braced on her knees. Her gaze followed a twig tossing and tumbling on its way downstream. That's exactly how she felt—carried along by forces out of her control, trying her best not to be sucked under by the current of life.

She rummaged in her saddle bag for the book and pencil she carried with her everywhere. Mom gave her a small, clothbound volume with blank pages every year for Christmas. Throughout the year, Ruth filled the pages with her most private thoughts and wonderings. Poems often took shape here, as well as a form of rhythmic prose she knew would horrify any true writer but which expressed feelings she couldn't describe any other way. Settling back on the rock, she began to write the phrases brought to mind by the helpless twig.

Who am I?
  Who do you think I am?
  Am I what you'd like me to be?
I'm just me, not entirely sure who that is.
Sometimes I say the right words, do the right deeds
Yet feel so empty

> wanting to know who I really am.
> Tired of pleasing
> > Wondering if I broke the shell
> > > would I still be worthwhile?
> Is what I feel the real me
> > Or just the me
> > Moulded by relentless circumstance?
> Why must I follow this stream
> > which changes with each season?
> I long for a predictable path
> > A future with no uncertainties
> > A present with no doubts
> > A past with no unanswerable questions.
> But that's impossible.
> And so, with no other choice
> I do my best to keep my balance
> Hoping the rapids I hear ahead won't suck
> > me under,
> Praying the waterfalls won't crush me,
> Sensing survival lies not in resisting
> > but in resting,
> Trusting that the One who controls the stream
> > will not forget me.

She read and reread what she'd written. The last line especially disturbed her. Where had it come from? Though she could remember kneeling by Mother's knee as a little girl and asking Jesus to be her Savior, she'd been keeping Him at arm's length for a long time. Now she wondered if she might be making a mistake. She closed her book as if to shut out the disquieting thoughts. Other matters needed attention, like how to handle the end of her days in the classroom.

Alone beside the creek, she could finally afford to let her feelings surface completely. Her school represented her place of value in this rural community. In just a few months, her place would be obliterated. She felt as useless as she had the day she'd watched her twin brother repeatedly sucked under by a relentless current. Though logic told her she'd be no less appreciated after the school closed, she still felt rejected and discarded. The future looked bleak because she could see no way of regaining the sense of worth teaching had given her.

What if she accepted Grandmother Carrington's offer? If nothing else, she could at least get her teaching certificate. It shouldn't take more than a couple of years. If she found city living tolerable, she could go on and maybe even get a university degree, perhaps go into nursing. Somehow the ideas stirred no sense of anticipation. At least they offered an option. A firm decision could wait.

Deliberately turning her thoughts to more casual matters, she munched a butter and honey sandwich as her gaze drifted up and down the creek bank. Just beyond a thicket to her left, the creek made several curves before it reached the beaver dam. The swampy area around those curves grew magnificent pussy willows. They wouldn't be ready for cutting just yet, but she'd have to remember to come back next week.

When she finally returned home, voices in the bush just beyond the corral indicated Greg and Phillip were improving their tree fort. This would probably be their last weekend of leisure. Spring planting would start soon, then gardening, and from there one farming activity would follow another until after the snow fell. She wrapped Sunset's reins around a corral rail before taking her pack bag inside.

Mom glanced up from butter churning. "How was your ride?"

"Perfect." Ruth felt a genuine smile creep across her face. "I still can't believe I actually have a horse of my own. Unless you need me here, I thought I'd go into town and visit Grandma."

"That's a wonderful idea. Would you mind taking a few things to her?" Mom always canned and baked more than the family could use so she'd have enough to give away. She rarely let any of her family make a trip to town without sending something to Grandma Lucy.

"How did I guess you'd ask?" Ruth teased.

"I don't know." Mom grinned as she lifted the dasher and peered into the churning crock. "If you're not in a hurry, I'd like to give Lucy a bit of this fresh butter."

"I'll even help you wash it," Ruth offered, using the hand pump beside the sink to fill a basin with cold water. Together they lifted the crock and poured the buttermilk into a large bowl.

Mom scraped whitish lumps of butter off the sides of the crock and plopped them into the water. "Do you think you'll stay for supper?"

"If you don't mind." Ruth mashed the lumps repeatedly with a large wooden spoon until the butter had formed a single large blob and no further milky streaks stained the water.

"Not at all. I think the visit will be good for both of you. You will make sure you're home before dark?"

Ruth chuckled. "You can tell Dad I'll keep Sunset on the road, and I'll make sure we have plenty of daylight in which to come back."

Mom's eyes twinkled. "You know I had to ask, so I can

tell Dad we did discuss it."

"I know. He's such a worry wart."

"Only because he loves us," Mom assured her unnecessarily. "I think I have everything together. Is this going to be too bulky?"

Ruth surveyed the bulging bag. "I think I can still get it strapped on behind my saddle."

"Then have a good time. I think I'll go rest a bit before the little ones get up from their naps."

With only a little difficulty, Ruth managed to get the burlap bag tied in place. She urged Sunset into a trot, but the bundle didn't slip. Approaching Dawson Creek from the northwest, she reined her horse to a stop. Town always made her nervous. After the railroad had arrived in January 1931, the quiet village had mushroomed into a bustling center of commerce. More people milled about town on Saturday than any other day. At least she didn't have any extra stops to make. Though the boarding house sat on one of the town's main streets, a circuitous route would keep her away from the busier areas until the last minute. She nudged Sunset into motion. "Let's go, big fellow."

Once on the main street, she hurried him along the two blocks to the boarding house, then around to the back, where she tied him loosely to a ring on the outside of the barn wall. Tapping at the back door, she called out, "Grandma! It's me, Ruth."

Through the screen she could see Grandma hurrying down the hall. "Of course it's you, girl. I saw you riding around from the front. What brings you to town this late in the day?"

"I just wanted to come for a visit. Mom sent this for you and asked me to give you her love." She handed over the bag, then hugged her white-haired friend. "I also wanted you to see my birthday present."

"What is it?" Grandma Lucy's eyes sparkled with interest.

"You have to come see," Ruth said teasingly. "It's outside, so you'll have to put on your mud boots."

Grandma set her bag on the floor. "This can wait. Let's go see this present of yours."

Ruth led the way back outside and around the side of the barn. "There he is."

"Isn't he a beauty?" Grandma breathed, slowly reaching out to stroke the horse's neck. "What did you name him?"

"Sunset." None of her ideas felt foolish when shared with Grandma Lucy.

"What a perfect name! I would guess you spent the entire morning riding him all over the countryside."

Ruth grinned. "Pretty much."

"Well, I'm glad your travels brought you in to visit me. Can you stay for supper?"

Ruth nodded. "I only have to make sure I'm back home before dusk, or Dad will start fretting."

"Well, then, come on into the kitchen and we'll see what your mother is giving me this time. Bless her heart! Bread, her special chokecherry jelly, fresh butter, and some cookies. That girl must think I don't know how to cook." Twinkling eyes belied her fierce words. She used a fork to test something in a steaming pot. "So where did you and Sunset wander?"

"Mostly down by the creek. He munched grass while I scribbled and thought. May I set the table for you?" Ruth felt awkward doing nothing while Grandma Lucy bustled.

"Thank you. There will be six of us. You know where

everything is. Do you mind telling me what you were thinking about?"

Ruth laid the plates, cutlery, and glasses in precise position while mentally searching for the right words. She knew from experience Grandma Lucy would wait patiently for as long as necessary. "Mostly about school," she finally confessed.

Grandma Lucy turned from her bread board to face Ruth. "You're having a tough time with it closing, aren't you?"

Ruth nodded without looking up.

"Are you ashamed of hurting?" The gentle tone enveloped the younger woman in compassion.

"No, but I wish I didn't feel this way."

Grandma Lucy didn't say anything, but her intense gray eyes invited Ruth to elaborate.

"I feel helpless. I'm losing a vital part of my life—" Ruth's voice cracked. She swallowed hard. "And there's nothing I can do about it."

"Have you thought about what you're going to do after June?"

"I don't see many options. Even if I had the skills for a different job, it wouldn't be the same as teaching. I can either make the best of helping out at home, or accept Grandmother Carrington's offer to go live with her."

Grandma Lucy only faltered a moment in her stirring as she poured canned peas into the pot of creamed potatoes. "Are you seriously considering a move to Toronto?"

"I don't know." Ruth swallowed around another lump in her throat. "In her last letter she offered to send me to one of the fancy schools there or to find me a husband."

"What do your parents think of the idea?"

"I haven't told them. When the letter first came, I just

put it away with all the others. Since I lost my job, though, the offer's become more attractive."

"It would be hard for you to live with someone who feels about your dad the way she does."

Ruth abruptly sat down on the chair at the end of the long table. "I hadn't thought about that."

"The day she arrived on the first train, she told everyone within earshot how she holds him responsible for your mother's death and how she intended to rescue her daughter's children from him."

"Every letter I've received from her contains at least one derogatory remark about him. I thought she was just writing those things to try to get me to come live with her."

Grandma Lucy placed the full bread basket and a bowl of butter on the table. Putting a hand on each of Ruth's shoulders, she looked straight into her eyes. "Please just promise me you'll let your Heavenly Father direct your decision."

Ruth wanted to give the answer that would make Grandma happiest, but she couldn't bring herself to say something she didn't mean. Boarders began gathering at the table, relieving her of the need to reply. Grandma stepped away from Ruth, but her eyes promised the discussion would continue later.

While helping put serving dishes on the table, Ruth recalled when Grandma Lucy had looked after only Mom and another boarder named Mr. Carey. When Mom had lived here, most of Grandma's business had come from farm families who had to stay overnight for various reasons. Since then, the house had been expanded to make room for a total of six residents. Dawson Creek's growth had filled Grandma's house with single men who'd come to find jobs but didn't want to live at the hotel. Gruff Mr. Carey still occupied his room to one side of the large kitchen. Only three others settled around the table, though Ruth guessed the vacancies would fill quickly. All four waited for Grandma to ask the blessing before helping themselves to the steaming chicken and potatoes. After multiple helpings and two pieces of pie each, the men vanished to their rooms or outside.

Grandma submerged a stack of dishes in hot water and Ruth grabbed a dish towel. Grandma tried to scowl, though her merry eyes marred the effect. "I can handle these. You just relax. I remember what teaching can do to a body. Ida used to come in looking like she'd wrestled a grizzly."

Ruth grinned but didn't relinquish her dish towel, secretly relieved Grandma had forgotten the earlier sensitive discussion. "That's what I feel like some days. Anyone who doesn't think spring fever exists ought to stop by my schoolhouse this time of year."

"Do you remember how Nettie Harper used to create a ruckus? Your mom used to come home almost in tears."

"It's hard to believe she's married and due to be a mother soon."

Grandma laughed. "Young Jeff Williams is braver than I expected of any fellow his age. Being loved has settled Nettie a lot, though. I expect motherhood will do the rest." She gave her dishcloth a good wringing, then snapped it out of the twist. "Thanks to your help, we're finished already. How about a cup of your favorite tea?"

"I've been waiting all day for one."

"Ida used to love my peppermint tea, too. You remind me a lot of her when she lived with me."

Ruth felt her eyes widen in surprise. "How?"

"She was still making peace with her mother's death. During her first year of teaching, her life took a few unexpected turns, and like you, she felt she had to handle them alone. After awhile, though, she learned to take God's Word at face value when it says all our steps are ordered by the Lord."

As often happened in discussions with Grandma Lucy, Ruth felt like the protective layers around her heart had been peeled back and its secrets revealed. Yet in the process, she also felt thoroughly loved. It gave her courage to say what she couldn't have told anyone else. "My life makes Him look like a pretty lousy planner."

Grandma's rough-skinned hands grasped Ruth's smooth ones gently. "He has given you a lot of heartache, child. I like to think it means He's also given you a capacity for more joy than most people discover. The times we can't explain why His plan is the way it is are our greatest opportunities to trust Him. Nothing brings Him greater joy than our trust even when we hurt."

Ruth dared to look into her friend's eyes. "I don't think I could do that."

A mysterious smile lit Grandma Lucy's eyes. "I've felt that way, too. If you want to hear about it, ask Ida to tell you my story some day. The most important lesson of my life, and one it seems I have to relearn almost every day, is that trust isn't a feeling. It's a choice. It's probably the most difficult decision we ever make. Every time God sends us something we don't understand, we have to choose again."

What she talked about sounded wonderful, but too far removed from where Ruth lived. "It still sounds impossible."

"I know, dear. But if you ask our Father to show you the way, He will." Returning from the stove where she'd put more water on to boil, she pulled Ruth into a long hug.

Ruth let herself relax in the embrace. She thought she heard Grandma whispering, but she couldn't be sure.

Though their conversation moved on to family activities and community events, Ruth's mind returned to Grandma Lucy's *"Trust is a choice"* as she rode Sunset home. Obviously Grandma didn't understand the depth of her problem. God's involvement in the life of Ruth McEvan had been sporadic at best, nonexistent at worst. How could she ask Him for anything? Though she dismissed the idea as ludicrous, something deep inside ached to try it anyway.

six

"Dad, may I please be excused?" Greg sat on the end of the bench awaiting release from the supper table. Phillip had already bolted. Reportedly, they had just "two more things" before the tree fort would be perfect.

"In a moment, son. Phillip, please come back." Dad's eyes glowed with mystery and somethingelse Ruth couldn't define.

Phillip groaned loudly, but returned. "Sorry, Dad."

"You know better than to leave without being excused. But I have something more important to discuss. Please take your seat." He waited until the boys had settled. "Your mom and I have some special news for you. In about four months, you'll have a new brother or sister." He could hardly finish his sentence around his wide grin.

Ruth looked closely at Mom. "Is this why you've been so tired? I was beginning to think you were really sick."

Mom's smile matched Dad's. "I kept telling you it was nothing to worry about."

"Can we go now?" Greg looked bored.

Dad shook his head. "No. I need to explain something."

Ruth knew what was coming. They'd heard the same speech before Timmy and before Beth. Ruth, Phillip, and Greg would have to be sure to help Mom all they could so she wouldn't work too hard.

Dad had only said a few words before Ruth realized the speech had been rewritten. "Boys, I'm going to expect you to help your mother. I don't want her getting overtired. Ruth has enough to do with school, so I'm going to be watching you two. Until this baby is born, I don't want to hear your mother ask you to haul water, bring wood for the stove, or dump the slop pail. I want you to see what needs to be done and do it. No excuses. If I catch either your mom or your sister doing something you should have done, or having to ask you to do it, we'll have an immediate meeting behind the barn. Understood?"

"Yes, sir," the boys chorused.

Dad studied Phillip's face for several moments before dismissing the two. "I'm not sure he heard me," he muttered after the door slammed behind them. "But he's going to learn responsibility this summer or else."

Ruth laughed at his determined expression. "His teacher will thank you." She pushed down the familiar feeling of loss.

Her struggles increased as the days slipped away. Young Lionel, David and Tommy Spencer, Teddy Harper, and Phillip disappeared from the schoolhouse to help with planting. Ruth knew she wouldn't see them in her classroom again and had to blink back selfish tears. The students who were left absorbed her mood. By Friday, she realized she had to do something to lift them all from the doldrums. She rang the bell to call them in from lunch recess, but didn't write any assignments on the blackboard. When everyone had settled into their seats, she asked nine-year-old Tabby Spencer, "Do you know what will happen seven weeks from today?"

The girl's blue eyes sparkled from behind the white blond hair that always seemed to hang in her face. "Is that the last day of school?"

"Yes." Ruth tried to make her face reflect their excitement rather than her own heartache. "How would you like to plan a concert for that day?"

"But it's not Christmas!" Six-year-old Audrey protested. "We only have a concert for Christmas."

"That's what we've done before," Ruth explained gently, "but we can have a special program any time we want to work hard enough to make it enjoyable for your parents. What does everyone else think about the idea?"

The older girls exchanged glances across the room before Karin Harper, one of the thirteen-year-olds, asked, "What kind of concert?"

Ruth decided to take a risk. "Any kind you want."

"You mean we can plan it all ourselves?" Clara Spencer asked, her face alight with the challenge.

Ruth nodded. "Every Friday afternoon, I'll leave you to yourselves so you can plan or practice. I'll help as much as you want me to, but you'll have to ask. This will be entirely your project."

"Who will be in charge?" Julie Harper wanted to know.

"Whichever one of the older girls all of you pick." Maybe this part of her plan would prove to be a mistake, but she wanted the entire project to be their own.

After a few moments of silence, Sara Pierce raised her hand. "I think June should, since she's the oldest." Clara Spencer nodded agreement. Karin Harper didn't look so sure, but Ruth often had to mediate squabbles between the two sisters.

She looked at the fifteen-year-old, whose face showed interest for the first time all year. "Do you want to be in charge, June?"

"Yes, ma'am," the quiet girl replied. "It will be a lot of

work, but we can do it."

The rest of the afternoon flew by as the children discussed ideas. Ruth watched in amazement as June diplomatically coordinated everyone's suggestions into a workable plan. Even Greg, the only boy left in the classroom, responded well to her. Ruth tried not to wish they'd be back next year.

After the first Friday, Ruth felt comfortable leaving her students alone under June's supervision. She brought Sunset and a riding skirt with her to school the next week. Just as she'd suspected, the swampy area by the creek had produced some magnificent pussy willows. She trimmed off half a dozen branches, then made her way to the Pierce farm.

"What a pleasant surprise!" Mrs. Pierce exclaimed when she answered Ruth's knock. A stylish printed dress fitted her slender frame to perfection and not a hair had drifted out of its place in the elaborate arrangement at the back of her head.

Ruth held out her gift. "These are from Theo and me."

The lady's eyes misted, though she smiled with delight. "I know for sure it's spring when you bring me pussy willows. You two never forget. Can you stay for tea?" She rubbed one of the puffs against her cheek.

"For a little bit. June Harper is supervising a special project they're all working on, so I try to make myself scarce on Friday afternoons."

"You know you're welcome to come visit me any time you want." Mrs. Pierce put her willow branches in a cut glass vase that reflected sunlight in delicate rainbows and placed the vase in the middle of the dining table in the formal dining room. "You make me feel almost like Theo's home again."

"I miss him, too," Ruth admitted. "Has he written anything to you about when he'll be back?"

Mrs. Pierce filled a small flowered china plate with brownie squares. "He'd hoped to be home for a couple of weeks this summer, but he isn't sure if it will work out. He's now in charge of all the first-year students."

"That's wonderful." Ruth felt so proud of her friend she wanted to cheer. She watched her hostess fill tea cups from a graceful silver tea service. "I never doubted he'd make a terrific doctor."

"Me either." The mother's eyes glowed. "Apparently the hospital has also offered him a full-time job in the fall. I've been hoping he'd be able to set up a practice here in town, but I try not to interfere in his decisions. I know he'll make up his mind only when he's sure of what God wants him to do."

Sipping her tea, Ruth searched for an appropriate response. She envied her friend's confidence in God's direction.

"Do you have any plans for after the school closes?"

"Just helping out at home, for now." She tried to sound far more cheerful than she felt.

"Your parents are blessed to still have you around. I've realized lately my daughter will probably be setting up her own home right after she finishes school."

"Are she and young Lionel that serious already?" Ruth suddenly felt aged.

Mrs. Pierce refilled their cups. "I don't know, but he's exactly the kind of young man her dad and I have been praying for. We've prayed for Godly mates for our children ever since they were born."

After sending her students home that afternoon, Ruth lingered at the schoolhouse. Had her parents been praying for her future husband, too? Lately, her thoughts had turned more often to the possibility of marriage. She had no idea what kind of person she'd like to spend the rest of her life with, or if she'd ever be given the choice. Theo had been the only boy she'd spent much time with, at least until recently.

Since her birthday, Jed Harper had stopped by the McEvan farm at least once a week. She wondered how he found the time with all of his own responsibilities. The first couple of times, he had helped Dad finish training Star. At the boys' invitation, he had inspected the tree fort and pronounced it a fine piece of work. Mom remained the only one who could beat him at checkers. After awhile, his visits developed a routine. Timmy and Beth would see him coming and run to meet him, knowing he'd have a piece of candy or a whittled toy. Then after he'd visited with the family for awhile, he'd ask Ruth to accompany him on a horseback ride. They'd race down the road, Sunset matching Jed's stallion stride for stride. By the time they'd returned, Mom and Dad would have disappeared into their room. Gradually Jed and Ruth's conversations over the kitchen table had become longer. She'd learned of his determination to help his dad make their horse ranch the best in the Peace River Country and of his love for their land. While she hadn't felt comfortable disclosing her inner contemplations, she had found it easy to talk with him.

She swept the floor and tidied the shelves in preparation for Sunday. About a year ago, their Sunday fellowship had grown too large for the one-room cabin at Spencers' farm, so meetings had moved to the schoolhouse. Families took turns arriving early enough to move desks to the perimeter of the room and set up benches brought from the cabin. Lars Harper had enlarged the top of the wood stove so food could be kept warm until time to eat. One thing hadn't changed—children still outnumbered adults. Grandma Lucy and the Albertsons were the only adults without youngsters. The Millers, on the other hand, had added five between the ages of 5 and 21 to the gathering. Ruth had tried to befriend their eldest, Ellen, but the girl was too shy. She seemed happiest when left alone with the little ones.

Two days later, Dad's question during breakfast surprised Ruth. "Can anyone tell me what special day this is?"

Mom waited a few moments for someone else to speak up, then suggested, "Easter Sunday."

Dad gave her his special just-for-you smile. "Who can tell me what Easter means?"

"It's the day Jesus came alive again," Greg answered as he reached for another piece of bread.

"Phillip, can you tell me why that is so important to us?"

Phillip looked unusually contemplative. "Because only God could make that happen?"

"Excellent answer. Jesus said he was God, and that he would live again after he was killed. If he hadn't done so, that would have made him a liar. We would have no reason to trust God, and no reason to celebrate today."

There it was again—that idea of trusting God. It refused to leave Ruth alone. She tried to ignore it while she helped Mom dress the little ones for church. During the meeting, one person after another spoke about what Easter meant to him. She simply couldn't share their joyful emotion. As a younger person, the special day had brought her as much delight as anyone. Somewhere in the last couple of years, however, an unbridgeable gap seemed to have formed between her and the One she'd been taught to call Heavenly Father. Real communication with Him had become as remote a concept as flight. She both longed for and feared the awareness of Him she saw in those she met with each Sunday. Mr. Spencer's final "Amen" gave her respite from her mental debate.

Justin Harper appeared just as the ladies were cleaning up after lunch. He smiled charmingly at everyone, then drew Ruth outside. "A friend of mine wants to take a motor trip to Grande Prairie this afternoon and invited me along. Please say you'll come, too."

She shook her head. "We're going on a picnic with the Spencers and Pierces this afternoon. I'm sure you'd be welcome if you wanted to join us."

He snorted. "Sorry. Not interested. Jed's not going to be there, is he?" He glared at his cousin, who was exchanging farm talk with the other men.

She let astonishment show in her voice. "Why should he be?"

"I've heard about you two galloping around the countryside." His tone remained nonchalantly superior. "You must like him a lot if you'll put up with him making you ride a horse."

"But I like to ride," she protested. "Besides, I can't recall it being any of your concern."

"Just wait. One of these days. . ." With that enigmatic threat, he scrambled astride his swayback mount and headed back toward town. She returned inside, hoping no one had noticed the exchange.

"What did that boy want?" Kate Harper's voice seemed

to fill the schoolhouse. "How James and Ruby managed to raise such a useless dandy, I'll never know. Ruby keeps hoping he'll move back home, but I always tell her she's lost him for good. Probably should've had more paddlings when he was young. Take my Nettie, for instance. Now there was a difficult child if I ever saw one. But her pa and I never let her get away with a thing, and now she's a married lady with a baby due just any day."

Ruth caught Mom's glance and suppressed a smile. They'd often laughed privately at how much Nettie resembled her mother, and how Mrs. Harper turned every conversation toward the new baby. "At least it keeps her out of other people's business," Dad had observed drily. Mrs. Harper tossed a basin of water out the door, then rounded up her husband and sons and departed, keeping up a continuous stream of comments about the joys of being a grandparent.

"It always seems so quiet when she leaves," Ruth whispered to Mom.

Mom grinned. "Kate's actually very warmhearted. She's genuinely interested in other people, though she usually expresses it in words first, then actions. If someone needs help, she's always right there."

"Talking them to death," Dad muttered. "What time are we supposed to meet Spencers?"

Mom, Mrs. Pierce, and Mrs. Spencer debated the question for several minutes. The other two ladies wanted to make sure Mom had enough time for a nap. Mom didn't want to inconvenience the men's choring routines. Eventually, they agreed to meet at the pasture just behind McEvans' farm. "That way you won't have to walk far," Mrs. Pierce explained.

Mom protested. "I'm not an invalid."

"Not as long as you behave yourself." Dad put his arm around her shoulders. "Let's get you home so Nina and Cynthia don't get after me for not making sure you get enough rest."

While Mom rested, Ruth put Timmy and Beth down for naps, then prepared the family's picnic. The woodbox stood almost empty, but she remembered Dad's warning about what would happen to the boys if she filled it. Her mind drifted back and forth between Justin and Jed, comparing and contrasting them. Each had become a friend of sorts, though neither knew her as well as Theo. What fun they'd have this afternoon if he were around!

Grandma Lucy and Michael Harper came with Spencers, increasing the gathering to a whopping eighteen. Grandma and Ruth took Timmy and Beth for a walk by the creek while the other three ladies sat on a blanket and visited. When Ruth and Grandma came back, the men had been lured into playing freeze tag with the older children. Little Audrey even managed to tag her dad and Mr. Pierce. By the time the ladies set out the food, everyone had worked up an appetite.

"This is certainly a nice break from the fields," Mr. Pierce observed. "Who made these wonderful jelly sandwiches?"

"I did." Ruth felt herself blushing. "But Mom made the jelly."

He waved what was left of the sandwich toward Dad. "Your wife's almost as talented as my Cynthia."

"Don't I know it." Dad patted his stomach. "She's fattened me right up."

Talk drifted to recipes among the ladies and seed prices among the men. Ruth let the words float around her, not really listening to any of it. She felt isolated from both the adult conversations and the children's activities. She busied herself gathering picnic remnants and putting them in the appropriate containers to be taken home.

Young Lionel approached his dad. "May Sara, Michael, Clara, and I walk home?"

Mr. Spencer's eyes lit with teasing twinkles. "If you need exercise, we have plenty of rock-picking to do."

Young Lionel blushed. "Dad!"

Mr. Spencer relented. "You'll need an adult with you. If Miss McEvan is willing to chaperon, you may go as far as Sara's place. We'll pick you up there."

Ruth relished the opportunity to do a little teasing of her own. "Sure. I'd enjoy visiting with the girls." Clara and Sara both turned pink. Until this afternoon, she hadn't realized Jed's younger brother was sweet on Clara Spencer. Junior romances seemed to be springing up everywhere.

Her mind turned introspective again as she followed a discreet distance behind the two couples. She'd never felt like looking at anyone the way these kids looked at each other. Though Sara was only 13 and Clara merely 14, Ruth wouldn't be surprised to see marriages in a couple of years. There was an indefinable something shared between each couple that carried a hint of forever. Sort of like the seed form of the way Dad and Mom looked at each other.

It felt strange to be considered a suitable chaperon. The more she thought about it, the older she felt. Why hadn't she ever experienced the springtime love she now supervised? Had she missed an opportunity that would never return? If love had come into her life, she wouldn't now be facing an empty future.

They had just reached the edge of the Pierce farm yard

when Ruth heard the rattle of the Spencers' wagon. She declined the offer of a ride home. Early evening sun still provided plenty of light, so Dad shouldn't mind her walking alone.

He was leaning against the corral when she arrived. "Have a good walk?"

"Sort of." She wondered if he'd been waiting for her.

He didn't leave her in suspense long. "Care to talk about what you've been thinking today?"

She leaned against the rails, too, so she wouldn't have to look at him. "Nothing makes sense anymore." When put into words, her feelings sounded ridiculous. "Following those kids home tonight, for the first time ever, I felt old. Isn't that stupid?"

He didn't laugh. "No, Ruthie, it's not stupid. You are older than most young people around here are when they get married. But it's nothing to be ashamed of. Ida was older than you when we got married."

"I know. But sometimes I wonder if I'll be an old maid living with you and Mom for the rest of my life." The words came out almost in a whisper.

He lifted her chin until she looked in his eyes. "If God arranges things so that you never leave us, I'll feel blessed. But I don't think that's what He has in mind. He's made you a unique and precious person, and He's been preparing an equally special young man to be your husband. Until then, don't you dare feel guilty for still living at home. Mom and I thank God every day for loaning you to us as long as He has."

"Really?" He'd said much the same thing after the trustees' meeting, but tonight his words soothed a sore spot deep inside. "I mean, I probably won't have a job next winter, and the house is going to seem pretty crowded when the new baby gets here."

"You'll never make us feel crowded, Ruthie. You bring us joy just by being yourself. Whether you have a job or not doesn't matter. You're family. You don't have to pay your way."

Though she returned his hug, she knew she'd only let him see the surface of her heartache. She couldn't bring herself to tell him how worthless she felt, how much anger she'd harbored since the river, how desperate she'd become in her search for escape from her own feelings. "Do you mind if I go for a short ride?"

"If you don't stay out too long. You don't want Sunset to trip over any dead logs or into any holes."

Once on the road, she urged Sunset into a gallop. Though she hadn't mentioned it to Dad, Justin's remarks had added to her emotional tangle. Should she tell him not to call on her anymore? But then he'd assume she and Jed were getting serious. Why couldn't he be as considerate and uncomplicated as Theo? Though she couldn't find the words for a letter, if there were any way she could actually talk with Theo, she knew he'd help her find a solution.

seven

Justin made another appearance Tuesday evening to ask Ruth to accompany him Friday to a Shakespeare reading. *This might be a good way to find out if he's really as obnoxious as he seems,* she thought. Except for the ride into town and back home, they'd be among a crowd. Besides, she relished the prospect of hearing classical literature. On the appointed evening, she stood ready and waiting when Justin arrived. She had chosen one of her longer skirts, a navy blue one with pleats, and a long-sleeved cream-colored blouse with a navy and green tie at the neck. A matching scarf held her hair away from her face. Since she wouldn't have to do much walking, she chose her dressy school shoes instead of boots.

"Maybe you should take your coat," Mom suggested. "That gray sky looks like it could get cold tonight."

Ruth grabbed the garment off its peg by the door, blew Mom a kiss, and hurried out to the buggy. For some reason she couldn't define, she didn't want Dad talking to Justin for long. Justin helped her into the buggy, then encouraged the team of horses to navigate the lane more quickly than was necessary. Ruth wondered where he'd borrowed the assemblage. His own horse was a sad-looking creature of indeterminate parentage, offered by a trader who had realized Justin's ignorance of horseflesh and dedication to a bargain. "Guess what I heard today? We're going to start getting mail by aeroplane rather than train. They're saying it will come in once a week regular-like now."

"I thought it's always come in weekly," Ruth ventured, feeling her inadequate knowledge of town routines.

"Well, it's supposed to," he replied in a tone laced with sarcasm, "but you know those trains. If they're not late, they're too full, or some such thing. Aeroplanes are real progress, that's for sure. Another couple of years, and they'll completely replace trains."

Ruth could tell he didn't really know what he was talking about, though it felt good that he wanted to impress her. Before she had time to think of any kind of reply, he launched into a description of the automobile he hoped to buy. "They're so much cleaner than horses," he explained. "Besides, you don't have to feed or water an automobile. Just park it and forget about it until you need it again."

"Isn't it expensive to buy?" Ruth queried.

Justin waved a hand carelessly. "With the kind of money I plan to be earning in the next few years, the cost of a car would be pocket change."

"I didn't realize the telegraph office had become so successful." Ruth now felt genuinely interested. If the telegraph office were prospering, then many other businesses in Dawson Creek would be, too. That would mean better prices for farm produce, which would benefit many families she knew.

"It is getting busier, but that doesn't mean anything to me. I'm looking for a really good job. Hopefully I can get something at the airport and then learn to fly some day. With my own plane I could fly wherever I wanted and get rich doing it." He laughed loudly and slapped the reins to make the horse trot faster.

His arrogance stunned her. He obviously thought life would give him whatever he wanted. She wondered why he wanted to spend time with her.

The reading turned out to be as entrancing as she'd hoped. Two town teachers, Miss Riley and Mr. Bentworth, performed together from several different plays. They read their parts so convincingly Ruth felt as though she were sitting in a city theatre rather than a small town schoolroom. Only Justin's obvious boredom marred her enjoyment. He sighed often and fidgeted, finally pulling a deck of cards from his pocket and laying out a game on his leg. She wanted to sink into the floor with embarrassment. When the final applause faded, she picked up her coat and stalked outside. He followed quickly, pleading for an explanation.

As soon as they opened the door, Ruth realized a more serious problem had developed. The gray clouds Mom had noticed had been harbingers of a spring snowstorm. Huge, fluffy flakes drifted thickly out of the sky, driven into swirls of whiteness by a biting wind. Some of the snow had melted already, creating trails of mud where streets had been. Traveling home would be slow and cold.

Justin's face paled when he saw other wagons and buggies struggling through the mud and accumulating snow. "I guess I won't be taking you home tonight."

She looked at him in shock. "What do you mean?"

"I've rented this buggy from the livery. What if I get all the way out to your place and can't get home again? I'll have to pay for an entire extra day." His expression indicated he couldn't believe she hadn't figured it out for herself.

"But, Justin, my parents will worry when I don't come home."

"Nah." He waved again in the careless gesture that now irritated her. "They know you're with me, so you're perfectly safe. They wouldn't expect me to bring you home in this mess. We'd both freeze, not to mention what would happen if the buggy slid off the road."

Ruth didn't trust herself to speak. If she were driving, she knew they'd make it. It would be cold, for sure, but at least they'd get there. However, Justin's pride would never let her handle the reins. With him guiding the horse, they probably would end up stuck along the side of the road. "I don't suppose you'd be willing to ride out to the farm and let my dad know I'm all right."

He shook his head with surprise. "If it's too cold to ride in the buggy, of course it's too cold to go on horseback. It's not a big deal, Ruth. I'll explain everything tomorrow."

But in the meantime, Dad would be half sick with worry. There was no way this selfish oaf would be able to comprehend. "Fine. Go wherever you need to go. I'll walk to the boardinghouse."

"Now, Ruth," he reached for her hands, but she pulled them back. "Don't get yourself all worked up. I'll give you a ride to the boardinghouse since it's on my way to the livery anyway. If your dad doesn't come into town tomorrow, I'll make sure you get home."

His patronizing tone sparked her anger. "Justin Harper, I've had it with you. Don't bother inviting me anywhere ever again. Your selfish arrogance is appalling. As long as we're on the subject, you mortified me in there tonight. If you didn't want to listen like a gentleman, why did you even go?"

He seemed to think she wanted an answer. "Because I

wanted to be with you." His tone sounded sulky.

"Then it's time you discover you can't have everything you want. I mean it. Don't come around again."

"At least let me give you a ride to the boardinghouse," he pleaded. "Everyone's going to see you walking alone, and they're going to blame me."

"Which is as it should be. Good night, Mr. Harper." She snugged her coat around her chin and set off toward Grandma Lucy's. Within a couple of blocks, she almost regretted her decision. On the gravelled sidewalks, wet snow lay deep enough to melt into her shoes. When she had to cross the road, mud sucked at her feet, making it almost impossible to walk. The wind whipped snow into her face and numbed her hands. She hadn't seen Justin driving past, so he must have sneaked to the livery by a back way. Angry indignation warmed her enough to get her to the boardinghouse.

The door swung open before she had a chance to knock. "Ruthie, child! Whatever are you doing out in this? Come inside and get warm before you even try to talk. Why, you're just about chilled through. Let's move this chair right close to the stove. Now sit, and I'll take off your shoes. Put your feet here in this pan of warm water. I'll run upstairs and get a comforter to put around your shoulders." Grandma matched actions to words, peeling off Ruth's soaked coat, pouring steaming water into a basin, and tucking the blanket under Ruth's chin.

As warmth seeped into her chilled body, tears began to trickle down Ruth's cheeks. "He wouldn't even ride out to tell Dad where I am." She gulped back a sob of exhaustion.

"Who wouldn't, dear?" Grandma held a cup of hot tea,

her antidote for any crisis, toward her. "Drink this, and tell me what happened."

Ruth took a sip of the honey-and chamomile-flavored liquid. "Justin. He asked me to come with him to hear Miss Riley and Mr. Bentworth read Shakespeare." Another sob welled in her throat, but she washed it down with tea. "He spent the entire evening fidgeting like a first-grader. He even pulled out a deck of cards, Grandma! It was so embarrassing, and he didn't even care." The sob made it all the way out this time.

Grandma set the tea on the table nearby and gathered Ruth into her arms. Held against Grandma's loving warmth, Ruth let tears take over. When her weeping quieted, Grandma asked, "How did you end up walking here?"

Ruth pulled back so she could look into Grandma's face. "The storm started while we were inside. Justin said it was too cold to take me home and that he didn't want to get stranded out at the farm because he'd have to pay extra for the horse and buggy he'd rented. I know Dad's just going crazy worrying about me. He always does when I'm out after dark."

"Did he just leave you at the school?" Angry glints showed in Grandma's eyes.

"No. He wanted to give me a ride here because he was afraid people would see me walking alone and blame him for abandoning me. I told him he deserved to be blamed, and that I didn't want to see him ever again."

Grandma stroked Ruth's drying curls. "I guess this red hair isn't just for show."

Ruth felt a smile appear. "When he told me my dad shouldn't worry, my temper took over. My reaction wasn't at all Christian or ladylike."

"But it was perfectly human." Grandma handed her the tea again. "Justin didn't treat you with respect, and it's a healthy sign that it made you angry."

"What do you mean?"

"Sometimes a young woman gets so desperate for a husband, she lets a young man treat her inconsiderately. It may be like Justin not caring about your feelings tonight, or it could be more obvious, like making fun of her or treating her as though she can't think for herself. Unfortunately, he'll only get worse after marriage. That's how women end up marrying men who hit them. As long as a man's disrespect makes you angry, you won't marry the wrong kind of person."

"Is there any way to let Dad know I'm okay?" Ruth knew he'd probably begun to pace. The storm had come from the north, which meant it would have hit the farm before town. He'd know exactly what kind of weather she'd been out in.

"Are you goin' to jabber all night, Miz Barry?" The door on the right side of the kitchen opened, and Mr. Carey's rumpled head emerged.

"I don't know, Mr. Carey. Ruth McEvan has been stranded in town and we were trying to figure out a way to get word to her dad that she's with me."

He scowled. "She didn't come in with her family?"

Ruth looked at Grandma, wondering what she'd say. Grandma paused. "A young man brought her in for the Shakespeare reading, but his horse isn't very surefooted in this weather."

"If that Harper boy is the one, the problem ain't his horse. How do you think your horse would manage?"

"Morton's steady in any kind of weather."

"If you'll let me ride him, I'll take a message out to the farm then."

"Would you really? Oh, Mr. Carey, you're just wonderful." Relief warmed Ruth all the way through. Stepping out of the pan of warm water, she impulsively ran to hug him.

He squirmed away, though his eyes looked suspiciously soft. "Ain't no cause for carryin' on. Just hate to know a man's all worked up over nuthin'."

Grandma Lucy almost hid her grin. "Do you have a good rain slicker? That snow's melting almost as fast as it's coming down and there's a sharp wind. You'll also need a good wool sweater underneath. I can wrap up a jar of hot coffee to give you something warm to drink on the way and—"

Mr. Carey held up his hand. "Just 'cuz I'm offerin' to do Miss McEvan a favor doesn't mean I need you runnin' my life. I wouldn't huv offered if I didn't know what I was doin'." His door shut with an emphatic click.

Grandma Lucy grinned. "Isn't it a shame when a man has to work that hard to be a grump?" she whispered, emptying the coffee pot into a quart jar, which she wrapped in several dishtowels.

Ruth grinned back. "Mom's told me how he's mostly bark and very little bite."

"When it comes to you children, he's a genuine pussy cat, if you don't mind a different metaphor." She paused as he came out of his room wearing a wide-brimmed floppy hat and a slicker that reached past his knees.

"Got that coffee ready?" He harumphed when she told him to ride safely and thumped down the hall in his rubber boots.

"Did you know he still talks about the first time you visited here?" Grandma poured the pan of water into her slop pail and handed Ruth a fresh cup of tea.

"I'm not sure I remember," Ruth confessed.

"You and Ida had talked at church, and she brought you home for supper."

Ruth thought she recalled what had happened. "Wasn't that the day we went on a sleigh ride with a man who wanted really badly to impress her?"

Grandma nodded. "Ken Danielson. You were the first guest Ida had invited here. Mr. Carey commented after you left that you had the saddest eyes he'd ever seen. He always asks how you're doing, and was pretty mad when he heard your school is closing. I'll bet anything he was eavesdropping, and that's why he came out when he did."

"It was really nice of him to offer to ride out there."

"You should have seen the look on his face when you hugged him." Grandma giggled again. "I don't think anyone else could have gotten away with it."

"It's strange that he wants to be so nice to me. It's not like he's known our family for a long time or anything."

"It's not strange at all, dear girl. You and Ida both have gentle hearts which bring out the best in people. That's part of why you're such good teachers."

Ruth felt her cheeks warm at the praise. "At least a dozen times a day, I wish I had somewhere I could teach next fall. I'm still wondering if I could handle living in the city long enough to get my teaching certificate, maybe even a degree."

Grandma filled the teacups again. "You mean accept your Grandmother Carrington's offer?"

"Just for a couple of years," Ruth mumbled, looking

down into her tea.

Grandma paused. "Why?" Her uncharacteristically short answer surprised Ruth.

"I'm not sure there's anything left for me here," she admitted. "Dad says he and Mom are blessed to have me around, but I don't feel like a blessing. Without a job, I feel useless. Why should they have to support me when I'm supposed to be an adult, and they still have little ones?"

"It sounds to me like you're calling your dad a liar. In the process you're also calling God a liar."

Ruth couldn't deny the first part of the accusation, though she didn't see what it had to do with God.

"If you can't trust your dad when he says you're no burden, how do you expect to trust God when He says He's ordering your life?"

"I wish I could," Ruth mumbled miserably.

"May I tell you what I think?" Grandma waited for Ruth's nod. "I think you're still angry with God for allowing your mother and brothers to drown. Until He explains Himself, you aren't willing to give Him more than token trust. You're trying to control your life so well you don't have to depend on Him."

Again, Ruth wished she could contradict Grandma's statement.

Grandma placed her hands around Ruth's tight grip on the cup. "Please look at me, child. God understands your fear of trust. He knows you feel betrayed. But He'll only be your Lord as far as you'll allow Him. If you want to run things on your own, He'll let you until you realize how puny your understanding is compared to His wisdom." She let the words sink in before continuing. "Have you read the book of Job in the Bible?"

Ruth shook her head. "It always looked boring." In all honesty, she hadn't opened the covers of her Bible in months.

Grandma smiled understandingly. "You might not find it so boring now. Job was one of the wealthiest and one of the most righteous men in the world of his time. God let Satan take away Job's entire family, all of his possessions, his health, and his wife's loving support. Scripture says, 'In all this, Job sinned not, nor charged God foolishly,' and later, 'In all this did not Job sin with his lips'. Yet while he didn't blaspheme, he still tried to demand an explanation from God. God let Job yell into the wind as it were until he ran out of demands. Then God finally revealed Himself, but without explaining any of His actions. He merely gave illustration after illustration of man's complete inability to understand or explain God. Once Job traded his demands for an appreciation of God Himself, God rewarded him with twice as much wealth as he had had before, restored his health, and gave him a new family."

Ruth looked at Grandma disbelievingly. "You mean God did all that to Job just to make him trust Him?"

"No, that's one of the strange things about Job's story. What happened to Job was actually a result of Satan trying to prove that Job only loved God because God had blessed him. God knew Satan was wrong, so He let him take away the blessings."

"Did God ever tell Job why it all happened?"

Grandma shook her head. "Not as far as we can tell from Scripture. It's what I find so beautiful about the story. Through Job's experiences, God illustrated the value He places on trust. Trusting God means we have more confidence in who God is than in our ability to understand Him."

"But how can we trust Him if we don't understand Him?"

Grandma's eyes glowed as if imparting invaluable treasure. "We trust because we believe what God says about Himself. He says He loves us. He says He wants only what is best for us. So, even though we can't explain how He accomplishes those objectives through what we see as the bad things in our lives, we have confidence in His ability to do what He says. That's why trust has nothing to do with how we feel. It has everything to do with who He is."

Ruth studied Grandma's face for several minutes. "I wish I trusted God like you do. I've tried, but it just doesn't work."

Grandma's grip tightened around Ruth's hands. "My dear child, trust isn't something you try. It's something you just do. When you get desperate enough, you'll discover how easy it is. Now, let's get you to bed."

Long after she'd been tucked into the big double bed in the room beside Grandma Lucy's, Ruth lay staring into the darkness. Every time she closed her eyes, she could see the river. Against her will, she felt again the sickening thump of their raft hitting a submerged log then tipping them all into the water. She'd been holding baby Greg, so she swam to the bank and laid him on the grass. She'd turned back to the water in time to see Dad dive in after depositing Phillip. He'd hollered for her to stay put and watch the little ones. She'd watched Mother's head go under just before Dad reached her. Daniel had tried to help, but a piece of the raft struck him on the head and the current carried his limp body downstream. She screamed as she followed on the riverbank, useless to do anything. An eddy sucked him under, taking with him her childhood faith. Nine-year-old

Sam and seven-year-old Benjamin also vanished.

She buried her face in her pillow, trying to shut out the horrible memories. Instead, she saw Dad's grief-stricken eyes as exhaustion had forced him to give up his futile search. The look on his face had solidified her anger. It felt as though her heart had iced over. She didn't cry for almost two years. With the first bout of tears came enough healing to help her function again, but the rage hadn't dissipated. The incredible effort of maintaining her schooling while taking care of her family had been a relief. As long as she kept too busy to think, the horrible, helpless feeling stayed in the shadows. Teaching accomplished the same. Except she could no more preserve her classroom than she could have rescued her family.

Rage boiled inside. How could God do this to her again? She had to clamp her lips together to keep the screams inside. If only she were out on a ride with Sunset where she could let it all out. The urge to scream turned into sobs so intense, she felt the bed shake. Scalding tears poured down her cheeks. Only one word filled her brain. "Why? Why? Why?"

Only vaguely, she felt comforting arms scoop her against a warm shoulder. A tender voice gradually subdued her mental roaring, though she heard no specific words. Her weeping continued as though squeezed from her very soul. Gentle rocking finally replaced her tears with sleep.

eight

Sunlight peeking around the curtains woke Ruth the next morning. She studied the unfamiliar surroundings for several moments before remembering where she was. The reading, the storm, Mr. Carey's trip to the farm gradually came into mental focus. Then those tormenting memories after she'd gone to bed. Her eyes felt sticky and sore and her head felt swollen.

She dressed and bathed her face gently from a basin of cool water on a wash stand by the door. Grandma Lucy met her at the bottom of the stairs with a hug. "Did you sleep okay?"

Ruth's still fragile emotions produced more tears. "Yes, once I got to sleep. Were you in my room last night?"

Grandma smiled and nodded. "You fell asleep in my arms. It wasn't a nightmare that upset you, was it?"

"Memories." She saw understanding in the soft gray eyes. "I'm sorry I disturbed you."

Grandma gently brushed tears off Ruth's cheeks. "Please don't be. I only wish I could take away the hurt." After another hug, she asked, "Do you feel like breakfast?"

Surprisingly, she did. She'd just finished her third pancake drenched in cranberry syrup when Dad arrived with Mr. Carey in the mud-spattered wagon with Morton tied behind. The snow had melted, making the outdoors a sea of mud. She ran outside to meet him. He leaped down and hugged her so tightly she couldn't breathe. "I was so worried about you."

Ruth leaned back to smile at him. "I know. I was worried about your worrying."

He gave her a ghost of a smile. If he noticed signs of last night's turmoil on her face, he didn't comment. "We thought sure Mr. Carey had brought us bad news. What happened that Justin couldn't bring you home?"

Ruth gave a sketchy account of the previous evening's events, omitting Justin's behavior during the readings and her angry outburst. Dad's brows drew together in a deepening scowl, so she tried to finish on a positive note. "Grandma Lucy bundled me up next to the stove, and Mr. Carey volunteered to take a message out to you."

Dad didn't change his expression. "Mr. Justin Harper and I are going to have a talk."

Grandma Lucy chuckled. "From what I heard, your daughter already gave him a good dressing down."

"A second one won't hurt," he replied grimly. "I think I'll stop by the telegraph office on our way out of town."

From her vantage point behind Dad, Ruth saw Justin's face pale as they entered the building. He tried to smile charmingly. "I was just going for lunch, but William here will be happy to help you."

"Since you're leaving anyway, how about meeting me outside. I'm glad what I have to say won't interfere with your working time." Dad's voice held an ominous chill. "I wouldn't dally if I were you."

Dad had just helped Ruth back into the wagon when Justin approached hesitantly. "If you'll let me explain, Mr. McEvan. . ."

Dad cut him off. "There's nothing to explain, Mr. Harper. The moment you invited my daughter to accompany you,

you assumed responsibility for getting her back to me safely. Since you proved yourself totally incapable of handling that kind of responsibility last night, you will never be permitted to take my daughter anywhere for any reason. Am I making myself clear?"

"Sir, I didn't think you'd want me to bring her home in such dangerous weather."

"And what was your excuse for not riding out to tell me where she was?"

Justin had to think. "My horse isn't very surefooted in mud or snow."

"That's a lame excuse if I've ever heard one. What kept you away from the livery?" The sarcasm in Dad's voice sent shivers down Ruth's neck. When Justin didn't reply, Dad continued. "Your problem, Mr. Harper, is selfishness. You didn't bring Ruth home because you didn't want to make the effort. Don't bother coming around to change my mind. You won't be welcome." He climbed into the wagon and slapped the reins. "Good day, Mr. Harper."

Dad said nothing until they were almost home. "I hope you didn't mind my telling him not to come around again."

Ruth smiled reassuringly, relieved to see his temper abating. "I already told him I didn't want to see him again. He didn't believe me, though."

"He'd better have believed me."

Mom met them at the barn with a hug for each. "Are you okay, honey?"

"I'm probably better than Justin." Ruth grinned. "Dad really let him have it. Grandma accused me of having a red-headed temper, but she should have seen Dad."

Mom ruffled Dad's rusty hair. "If all he did was talk to Justin, he restrained himself admirably. He *was* threatening physical violence. What happened last night?"

Ruth related the story, this time in its entirety. "I don't know why he even took me. He certainly didn't appreciate the readings."

Mom raised her eyebrows. "Who knows? If yours and Dad's combined efforts haven't convinced him not to come calling again, nothing will."

Jed's visit later in the evening helped soothe Ruth's lacerated emotions. He gave Beth and Timmy countless shoulder rides around the house, then let Greg beat him at checkers. Ruth thanked him for his patience after they escaped outside for a walk. "You're even better with the little ones than Greg and Phillip."

A bit of pink tinged Jed's ears. "Teddy arrived just before my tenth birthday, so I learned early how to handle babies. I've always wished I'd grown up in a large family like Uncle James and Aunt Ruby's. I probably ought to get married pretty soon if I want to see that dream come true." He looked at her with odd intensity.

She glanced away toward Sunset galloping across the pasture beyond the corral. "I hadn't realized before how much a part of my life my own horse could become. Isn't his gait just terrific? I enjoy watching him as much as riding him. My dad sure knows how to pick a horse."

He followed the conversational distraction. "You should come over to our farm and see the entire stock. The new colts pick on each other and carry on like a bunch of children."

She turned to lean her back against the rails. "There honestly isn't much about the farm I don't enjoy. Even weeding the—" A plume of black smoke off to the west caught her attention. "What's that?"

Jed squinted for just a moment. "It looks like a fire near the Pierces. I'll saddle up if you'll go get your dad."

Ruth dashed toward the house, yelling long before she arrived. "Dad! Dad, come quick!"

Dad yanked the door open just as she reached it. "What on —" He glanced over her head and saw the smoke. "Oh Lord, please help us!" he prayed aloud, then grabbed his coat and boots. "Ida, it looks like there's a fire at or near the Pierces' place. Jed and I are headed over to help. Phillip! Front and center right now!"

"I'll come, too." Mom reached for her coat. "Greg can watch the babies."

"No." Dad's emphatic response stopped her. He put his hands on her shoulders and gentled his tone. "If you come, you'll try to help and get all worked up. I'd much prefer you stay here. Prayer will do more for us than water, anyway. For your sake and for our baby, please?"

Mom wrapped her arms around him. "You're right. Just keep yourself safe."

He kissed her quickly and joined Ruth outside. "Are you coming?"

"If you don't mind."

"Cynthia and Sara could probably use your comfort." He looked back toward the house and bellowed, "Phillip John McEvan!"

The name had hardly left his mouth when the front door opened. "Coming, Dad. What's up?"

"Fire at Pierces' place. We're going to need your help."

Even Phillip's face blanched. Fire presented a fearsome threat. In moments, a blaze could destroy a farmer's most expensive assets. Even if livestock were saved, hay, feed and many farming tools usually disappeared with a barn.

Despite firefighters' best efforts, flames could easily spread to other nearby buildings. Lumber to replace any structure didn't come cheaply.

Once onto the main road, Dad encouraged the horses into their fastest trot. The fire's glow intensified as they approached Pierces' farm, confirming their fears for their neighbors. Ruth visualized the lovely home which she knew as well as her own. Would there be anything left of it?

Dad turned the team down Pierces' lane, providing a full view of the disaster. Huge flames leaped and danced around what had been Doug Pierce's beautiful, two story barn. Mr. Pierce stood at the well in front of the house, filling buckets as fast as he could pull them up. Jed had already joined the fight, carrying the water across the farmyard. Mrs. Pierce used what looked like a wet sheet to beat at the ground where sparks ignited smaller fires between the barn and the house. Dad stopped the team at the edge of Pierces' farmyard, tying the horses to a fence rail. Phillip leaped from the wagon almost before it stopped moving and dashed forward to join Jed. Ruth scrambled down and took off toward the well at a run with Dad right behind her. "I'll send Phillip to relieve Doug at the well," he yelled. "You and Mrs. Pierce can help most by keeping buckets full and sheets wet," he yelled as he ran toward Mrs. Pierce.

A large washtub sat beside the well. Ruth grabbed a bucket Mr. Pierce had just filled and dumped its contents into the washtub. Phillip came back with another empty bucket. "Mr. Pierce, Dad says for me to take over from you."

With only a nod, Mr. Pierce snatched the two buckets he'd just filled and ran toward the fire. Jed returned to the well for more water, and Sara approached from the house with an armful of sheets. Instead of crackling comfortably like a bonfire, these flames roared. The noise sounded like it came from all sides. Mrs. Pierce relinquished her battle to Dad and joined Ruth at the washtub. Her hair straggled around her face, while the stylish twist at the back of her head sagged. Soot streaked her face and dress. Though she looked ready to drop from exhaustion, she didn't hesitate before lifting a dripping sheet from the tub and passing it to Dad.

Ruth had never been more impressed with her oldest brother than during that night. He pulled endless buckets of water from the well almost as quickly as they were used to fight the blaze. In sharp contrast to his often indolent attitude toward farm chores, tonight he didn't pause for even a moment in his grueling, yet monotonous task. She emptied yet another pail of water into the washtub. Mrs. Pierce passed dripping bedsheets and full buckets to the men and accepted empties and sooty linen.

"Jed, look out!" Mr. Pierce's shout made Ruth look toward the barn just as what was left of one of the outside walls burned loose from its supports and fell outward. She bit back a scream as Jed barely leaped clear of the deluge of coals and sparks. All three men converged on the spot to prevent the burning fragments from starting new fires.

The close call reminded Ruth how easily this crisis could turn to tragedy. In volunteering to help, Jed had risked his life. Part of her mind focused on the vital task at hand while another part contrasted Justin and Jed. Just twenty-four hours had brought out the worst in one and the best in the other. Though they were close in age, Justin still behaved like a boy while Jed was, without question, a man.

Darkness engulfed them, but they fought on in the light

of the flames. Ruth's muscles ached from endless effort. Tension knotted her stomach. Bit by bit, the rest of the barn collapsed. Miraculously, the men kept the fire from spreading across the yard.

Dad appeared beside the washtub, so Ruth thrust another sheet at him. He let it drop. "Thanks, Ruthie, but we've won."

"What?" She turned to grab another bucket from Phillip.

"The fire's out. You can stop."

She looked blankly around the farmyard. Moonlight shadowed rubble which still smouldered where the barn had been. Jed stood guard, while Mr. Pierce comforted his now-weeping wife. Sara's scared face peered out the door. "What about his stock?"

"He'd just put them out to pasture yesterday. He figures he won't need bedding hay or feed for them until fall. Basically he just lost the barn itself." Dad draped his arm over her shoulders. "We couldn't have done it without either of you." He grabbed Phillip as the boy headed toward the ruins. "Son, I'm proud of you. You came through like a man tonight."

Phillip just grinned and shrugged away, but Ruth noticed a bit of pride light his face.

Sara thrust a tray of glasses at them. "Cold water?"

"Thanks." Ruth took two. "I'll take one over to Jed." He didn't turn until she called his name. "Jed? Are you all right?"

"Yeah." He drained the glass. "I wish we could have gotten here sooner. A barn's tough to lose."

His empathy for the Pierces intensified the admiration she'd been feeling toward him all night. "Thanks for being here. You came close to getting badly hurt."

"Yah. We do what has to be done."

"I was really scared for you when I saw that wall falling."

He turned to face her directly. "You saw it happen?"

"Yes. I almost screamed."

"I didn't think I'd be able to get out of the way fast enough." He seemed to look for something in her face.

She felt compelled to say something. "I'm glad you made it."

"Yah." He nodded. "I've been thinking about the things I would have missed out on if I'd been trapped."

The intensity and length of the conversation surprised her. He'd never before been so willing to talk. She didn't reply, hoping he'd continue.

He let a pause linger. "I've always wanted a family of my own someday. After tonight, though, someday's not soon enough." He studied her silently until Ruth started to feel uncomfortable. "Um, Ruth," he cleared his throat. "Maybe I'm a fool for asking, but. . ." He kicked at some blackened wood. "I mean, this is probably the worst time possible to ask, but. . ." Gulping air, he spoke his piece in a rush. "What I mean is, do you think you'd ever want to marry me?"

nine

Ruth peered dumbly though the darkness at Jed. "Are you serious?"

"Yah." Jed's speech had taken on the flavor of his parents' Norwegian background. "It's time I have me a family."

She had an overwhelming urge to laugh and cry simultaneously. She'd despaired of ever receiving a proposal, much less discussing the matter beside the smoking remains of Theo's parents' barn. "Why are you asking me? Why not some other girl?"

He kicked at a charred piece of wood. "Most girls want to get away from farmin'. You said you love it. Besides, Ma has been tellin' me for a long time how much she'd like to have you as a daughter-in-law."

"You've talked to your parents about us?" Ruth couldn't decide whether to feel flattered or insulted.

"Yah. I know I haven't been callin' on you long, but we do get along real well. Pa said he'd give us a few acres to build a cabin on. It wouldn't be much to start, but we'd build on as we could afford it."

Ruth felt as if she were sitting on a runaway horse. What could she say that would neither commit her nor turn away this possibility? It wasn't that she didn't care about Jed. She'd just never thought of him as anything but a friend.

He didn't appear disturbed by her hesitation. "This is too fast, yah? Maybe you should think and tell me later."

She would have hugged him if she hadn't noticed Mr. Pierce approaching. "Thank you."

"I don't know what she's thanking you for, son, but my wife and I are deeply grateful for your help this evening." He gave Jed a hearty thump on the back. "Do you have time to come inside for a little refreshment? We shouldn't have to watch this anymore. No coals could survive in all that water we dumped."

Ruth relished her reprieve from the confusing intensity of Jed's inquiry. She carefully removed her muddy, soot-streaked shoes at the door. "I hope we won't make a mess in Mrs. Pierce's lovely house."

"If it weren't for you, our house might not still be here," Mr. Pierce replied. "Don't worry about it, please." He directed them to the dining room table, where Mrs. Pierce sat with her hands in a bowl of water.

Ruth hurried around Phillip. "How did you burn yourself?"

Mrs. Pierce smiled wearily. "It must have happened when I was helping Doug before you came. I didn't realize until after it was all over how much my hands hurt." She lifted them out of the bowl. Blisters that must have formed early in the evening had been torn open by her handling of the buckets and sheets. Now patches of raw skin lay exposed on both sides of her hands.

Ruth winced. "That must hurt."

"Some." Mrs. Pierce submerged them again.

Mr. Pierce emerged from the kitchen with a pitcher of water and a steaming tea pot. Sara followed with glasses and mugs. They both vanished into the kitchen again and returned with cake and small plates. "Let's thank the Lord," he suggested. "Heavenly Father, thank you for keeping us all safe tonight, and that the fire didn't spread beyond the barn. Thanks especially for these friends who saw our need and came to help. Bless them as only You can do. I also ask You to ease the pain in Cynthia's hands and bring quick healing. In Jesus' name, Amen."

Ruth felt bone-deep exhaustion set in while she ate. Yawns threatened to escape each time she opened her mouth for another mouthful of cake. Mrs. Pierce ate or drank little, preferring to keep her hands in the cool water.

"Do you have some ointment and soft cloths?" Ruth asked softly under cover of the men's conversation. "I could bandage your hands for you before I leave."

Mrs. Pierce's lovely, gracious smile appeared again. "I'd appreciate that. Doug tries to be gentle, but he doesn't always succeed. Sara," she caught her daughter's attention. "Would you please bring me the burn salve from the kitchen and the cloth strips from the upstairs cupboard?"

Obviously pleased to be able to do something for her mom, Sara hurried back with the supplies. Ruth spread the salve as tenderly as she knew how.

"Ooh, that feels nice," Mrs. Pierce breathed. "It's taking the sting out already."

"Where did you get it?" Ruth studied the unfamiliar container carefully, thinking it would be handy to have around their farm.

Mrs. Pierce turned her hands so Ruth could complete her ministrations. "Theo sent it soon after he started medical school."

"I'm glad it works," Mr. Pierce observed. "I think we'd better see if we can find someone to help you around the house for a week or so. I'd rather you didn't try to do very much until those burns heal."

"I wish I could disagree, but there isn't much I could do alone." The injured woman looked at her husband as though drawing invisible strength from him.

"I'll help," Sara protested.

Her dad hastened to reassure her. "I know you will. I'd just like to have another adult around. You have to keep up with your studies, and your mom's going to need a lot of personal help as well as housekeeping."

Ruth glanced at her dad, who nodded slightly. "I'd be glad to stay with you for awhile, if you'd like. I'll be at school during the day, but I'm usually home by four in the afternoon."

Mrs. Pierce's eyes lit up. "Would that work, Doug? She and Sara can leave lunch for you on the stove. I should be okay on my own while they're at school."

Doug smiled. "I think what my wife is trying to say is that she can't think of anyone she'd rather have. If you're willing to come, we'd both be grateful."

"When would you like me to move in?"

Mr. and Mrs. Pierce looked at each other in the wordless communication Ruth had often seen her parents use, then Mr. Pierce spoke. "How about late afternoon tomorrow? Bring your whole family over and we'll have tea. Jed is welcome, too."

Dad nodded agreement while pushing himself away from the table. "If Ida's feeling up to it, we'll be here."

"How's Ida doing these days?" Mrs. Pierce wanted to know. "I've not been able to visit with her as much as I'd like."

"She's still tired and not eating much, but she assures me she's fine. I won't rest easy until the baby's born."

"Isn't that the way it always is?" Mr. Pierce grinned and

draped a protective arm around his wife's shoulder. "This business of having babies is pretty terrifying from our angle." Ruth remembered Theo telling about the three babies who had died between his birth and Sara's, and how close his mother had come to death when Sara was born.

"True enough," Dad agreed. "She wanted to come with us, but I asked her not to."

Mrs. Pierce nodded. "I'm glad you did, Timothy. Fighting a fire is no job for a woman in her condition. We'd have had a hard time forgiving ourselves if anything had happened to your baby tonight."

"You're sure she can spare Ruth?"

Dad smiled directly at Phillip. "Absolutely. She'll have two strong boys who've already promised to help as much as they can. We'd best be on our way. My wife isn't a worrier, but she won't go to bed until we're home."

The clock indicated an hour past midnight by the time they unharnessed the horses and stumbled into their own house. As Dad had predicted, Mom had waited up for them. She had hot bath water waiting and insisted on inspecting each of them for burns. "How are the Pierces?" she inquired as Phillip stripped off his shirt and disappeared behind the curtain that turned their kitchen into a bathing area.

"Cynthia burned her hands pretty badly before we got there," Dad responded. "She won't be able to do much for the next week or two, so Ruth volunteered to stay with them until her hands have healed."

"Bless you, Ruth!" Mom looked at her with shining eyes. "Your generosity makes me so proud, and even makes me feel I'm doing something to help by extension. You're a daughter to make any mother proud."

Despite Ruth's weariness and the warm bath, sleep did not come easily. Her thoughts wouldn't turn off. What kind of answer would she give Jed? He wouldn't wait forever. What would the future hold for her if she said no? It almost felt as if she had to say yes if she didn't want to be dependent her parents for the rest of her life. Hardly any chance existed of a man more dependable than Jed coming into her life. She certainly didn't feel about him the way Mom did about Dad. Maybe she just needed to make the commitment and love would follow.

Not a besotted kind of love, she told herself firmly, pulling on her housecoat for a trip on tiptoe to the kitchen. *Just a steady, comfortable affection.* She sat at the table and sipped milk, willing her whirling thoughts into stillness. Instead, they turned to last night's conversation with Grandma. Who was the Bible character she'd talked about? *Job*. Ruth resolved to read his story sometime. Maybe next fall when she no longer had a classroom. Perhaps she'd be married by then. A sigh from her soul sounded loud in the silent room.

"Troubles?" Mom's whisper startled Ruth. Her slippers shuffled against the plank floor as she moved around the table to sit beside Ruth.

"Did I wake you?"

Mom hugged Ruth's shoulders. "No, you didn't, but thanks for asking. My bedtime snack seems to have given me indigestion. I didn't want to wake your dad with my discomfort. What's keeping you up?"

Ruth looked down at the table, trying to decide which of her mental puzzles to put into words. "Jed proposed tonight."

Mom moved her hand to rub up and down Ruth's spine.

"You don't announce that like a young woman who's in love."

"I don't think I ever will be, regardless of who might want to marry me."

"Why do you say that?"

"You and Dad love each other so much, it's like you're two halves of the same whole. If anything goes wrong with one of you, the other one hurts. I'd rather not be so tangled up with another person."

"Ruthie, that's what makes marriage such a joy! I wouldn't have married your dad if I hadn't known we'd become one in spirit as well as in name. The pain of oneness makes its joys even greater."

Ruth felt her tense neck muscles relax under Mom's tender massage. "Is that why Dad frets about you so much?"

Mom kept her chuckle barely louder than Ruth's question. "He worries because he's afraid of losing us. Love is a lot easier when one trusts the care of an omnipotent God."

"God doesn't always protect loved ones."

"I know." Compassion echoed in Mom's voice. "I'd still rather love completely while they're here."

One of the things that had drawn Ruth to this lady years ago had been Ida's loss of her mother just a few months before coming west. Her dad had died in 1917 during the Great War. Ruth had felt Ida understood her pain as no one else could. Tonight she realized they had very different perspectives. "I wish I could feel that way."

"Ruthie," Mom placed her hand around her daughter's, "you can't go on holding God accountable for events only He can explain. You'll just become miserable."

"Grandma told me the same thing last night." Ruth returned gentle pressure. "She said God wants me to trust

Him most when I can't understand Him."

"Scripture calls that faith, and says without faith, we can't please God."

In that case, Ruth knew it would be a long time before she'd be pleasing to God. Trusting Him until she understood why He'd taken so much away presented too great a risk. "I think I can sleep now. Besides, if I keep you up any longer, Dad will have my hide."

She felt Mom's smile as loving arms closed around her. "I'll keep praying for you."

"Thanks." She wasn't sure prayer would do any good, but it couldn't hurt.

Morning came far too quickly. Gentle shaking awakened her and she tried to force gritty eyes open. Mom's face hovered over her. "I'll be serving breakfast in about twenty minutes."

Ruth knew she dare not stay in bed even a moment after Mom left, or she'd fall asleep again. Why did she feel so sore and exhausted? Memory returned with increasing detail. Would Jed expect an answer today?

≈

Church made her feel like a hypocrite. She mouthed words to hymns, listened dutifully to testimonies, and bowed her head for prayer while wishing she didn't feel so detached.

She risked a glance across the room at Jed. He appeared totally involved in the worship service. Finally, Mr. Spencer closed with a blessing on their meal. Ruth kept a smile glued to her face as she helped the other ladies move lunch from the stove to the outside table.

"—a big, healthy boy," Kate Harper was saying to anyone and everyone. "Her Jeff came to get me about ten o'clock, and by three, it was all over. My Nettie didn't so much as whimper. She just buckled down and got the job done. They've named him Aaron Lars after his two grandpas. He definitely has his mother's chin—"

"We weren't the only busy ones last night," Jed observed, settling beside her on the bench. "How do you feel after working so hard?"

"Pretty good," Ruth lied. "How about yourself?"

"Not bad, though I won't be able to visit Pierces with you this afternoon. Mom wants us to take a family trip over to see the baby." He grimaced. "She and Nettie are going to expect me to say how cute he is. I like children, but only after they pass the baby stage."

She managed to laugh while noticing how closely Ellen Miller watched Jed. She waited for the stab of jealousy which never came. It wasn't that she felt secure in his affection. She simply felt. . .nothing. Forcing her attention back to Jed, she predicted, "Just wait until the first time he calls you Uncle."

"We'll see." He didn't appear convinced. "It looks like Ma's already packing up to leave. I wanted to let you know I won't be around much this week. We've got two fields to seed and half a dozen colts to start breaking. But you're welcome to come over any time. If you need me for anything, send one of your brothers over with a message and I'll make time." His unspoken message came through clearly.

Meeting his gaze directly, she smiled genuinely for the first time. "Thanks, Jed."

He lifted his hat in salute and swung himself up into his parents' wagon.

Her lunch had lost its appeal somewhere in the conversation. She sidled over to the slop pail where scraps were collected each week for the Millers' pigs and discreetly cleaned her plate.

The afternoon kept her too busy to think. While Mom napped, Ruth filled two pillowcases with clothing and underthings. Comb and brush set followed, along with her nightgown. Her Bible also went in as a final afterthought. She tied each cloth bag closed.

When Mom awoke, she insisted on assembling a crate of food. "It will make things easier on all of you if you and Sara don't have to do any baking right away," she informed Ruth, setting three loaves of bread on top of a paper bag full of cookies, several jars of canned vegetables, and two jars of chokecherry jelly. "At least you know you can serve Doug jelly sandwiches for any meal and he'll be happy."

Ruth answered with a laugh. "You're going to get everyone in the area addicted to your jelly."

"As long as you and your brothers bring me plenty of berries in the fall, we won't have a problem." She wedged a final jar into place. "I think we're ready to go."

The family piled into the wagon. Ruth followed on Sunset, who would help her get to and from school much more quickly than if she had to walk. At least that's what she'd told Dad. Her real reason lay in the feeling of freedom and independence the animal gave her. He remained the single element in her life that didn't prompt disquieting thoughts and uncomfortable questions.

ten

Monday brought one of Ruth's most frustrating days in the classroom. Sunshine streamed across desks and tempted her students to restless behavior. She searched in vain for the inner well of patience on which she'd come to rely. Instead, irritated reprimands left her mouth before she thought. Lunch time brought an immense feeling of relief as she sent everyone outside and put her head down on her desk.

She had to get control of herself. Taking her inner turmoil out on her students was unforgivable. Tears seeped out from under her eyelids as she wondered how to make amends. A rustling at the door caught her attention. A folded piece of white paper protruded from between the door and its casing. Wiping her eyes, she crossed the room to investigate.

"*To Miss McEvan*" read the outside. Ruth unfolded it. "*Dear Miss McEvan*," the short note began. "*I love you and wanted you to know. Sara Pierce.*" Tears coursed down her face in earnest. The gentle words eased her troubled spirit and gave her an idea for making up for this morning. For starters, she'd give the class an extra twenty minutes of lunch break.

Everyone seemed subdued when she called them in. Once they'd settled into their seats, she spoke softly. "Class, I'm sorry for being such a grouch this morning. Will you please forgive me?" Their ready agreement threatened to crumble her composure, but she held on. "Thank you. I think maybe we should do something different this afternoon." A rustle of excited whispers swept the room. "In case you didn't know, Mr. and Mrs. Pierce's barn burned down Saturday night. Mrs. Pierce burned her hands trying to put the fire out. Would you like to write pretty notes to tell her we hope she gets well soon?" Seven of the eight heads bobbed excitedly. "What's the matter, Greg?"

He mumbled with embarrassment. "Boys don't make pretty things."

Knowing her brother's handwriting, Ruth didn't dispute the issue. "Is there something you'd rather do?"

He pondered the matter. "I could make her a rock collection."

Karin Harper snickered derisively, but Ruth silenced her with a look. "If you arrange them nicely and write her a note telling her something about each one, I think she'd find it a very nice present. Don't bring too many, all right?" She couldn't imagine a young boy's rock collection anywhere in the gracious Pierce home, but she'd resolved to make this afternoon as enjoyable as possible for her students.

"I know." Greg nodded as he dashed out the door.

Clara Spencer's hand went up. "May we talk while we work?"

Ruth smiled, thinking this could turn out very much like a ladies' sewing club. "Let's arrange your desks in a semi-circle in front of my desk, so we can all visit while we work."

"Are you making a card, too, Teacher?" Tabby Spencer wanted to know.

"I wish I could." Ruth wrinkled her nose in a mock

grimace. "But I really should grade some arithmetic papers."

"That sounds boring," Tabby pronounced.

"Won't we make it hard for you to conc'ntrate?" Julie Harper folded her sheet of white paper in half.

Ruth smothered a laugh. Actually, their chatter would make her least favorite job bearable. "No. I'll enjoy listening."

"You could just mark them all 100 percent so you could draw with us." Tabby's suggestion sounded like something Phillip would have thought of.

Ruth marked a red X beside two of her brother's incorrect answers. He knew his multiplication tables well, but often did his quizzes in such a hurry he made careless mistakes. "What do you suppose would happen if you took the paper home and your dad noticed I'd let you get away with incorrect answers?"

"My dad wouldn't even notice." June drew colored curlicues around the perimeter of her creation.

"Why do you say that?" Ruth put her pen down to concentrate fully on the girl's answer.

She looked up frankly. "He doesn't notice any of our schoolwork. I don't know why he makes us go when Jim is the only one who matters."

Ruth couldn't think of a good reply. She suspected James Harper Sr. probably didn't make a fuss over his children's schoolwork because he didn't understand what they'd done. Jed's mother had once mentioned that James hadn't gone to school beyond the third grade. But explaining this to June would only antagonize her further. "Does your mother talk with you about your work?"

"Nah. She's too busy. It doesn't matter. I think school's

boring anyway. I'd rather be married and have babies like Patricia."

Her sentiment gave Ruth no feeling of surprise. Keeping the girl in school this year had taken a combination of encouragement from her teacher and insistence from her parents.

"I just tell Mama what we've done while we work," Julie offered, coloring a large orange sun at the top of her paper.

Ruth noticed June's eyes flash. She hastened to intervene before a family feud broke out. "I'm glad you've been here this year, June. The concert you're organizing is going to be the best we've ever had."

The compliment did the trick. Conversation shifted enthusiastically to details of the program. Karin and Julie planned to sing "A Mighty Fortress is Our God" together. "We have to practice in the barn right after school so no one hears us before the concert," Julie explained as she cut shapes out of colored paper. "I'm singing melody and Karin is learning to sing something else."

"I listen to Mrs. Pierce on Sunday and try to copy her," Karin explained, her cheeks turning pink.

"Would you mind singing for me?" Ruth asked, curious to hear what the two had done.

"We have to stand up," chatterbox Julie informed her.

Ruth nodded. "That's fine."

Julie moved to stand beside her teacher. "First we hum, like Mrs. Pierce showed us in music class." The two hummed in unison, then Karin's voice moved to a tentative harmony and the hymn began. Their blended voices sounded almost identical when in unison, and enhanced each other in harmony.

"That's beautiful," Ruth enthused when they finished.

"You both have lovely voices."

"Do I sound all right?" Karin's penchant for perfection brought worried wrinkles into her forehead.

"You have a real talent for music," Ruth reassured her. "Not many people could learn how to do that just by listening."

Karin still looked disturbed. "There are a couple of parts that don't sound right, and I can't figure out what's wrong."

"Maybe you could come home with me some afternoon," Sara offered. "Mom could help you and Dad would drive you home afterward."

Karin's face glowed. "Your mom wouldn't mind?"

Ruth blessed Sara for thinking of it. Even this morning, Mrs. Pierce had already begun to fret about feeling useless. She wouldn't be able to play the piano, but her ear for music could help the girls without an instrument. Ruth turned to June. "If anyone else wants to sing, I'm sure we could arrange for Sara's mom to help them, too."

June basked in the recognition of her leadership. "I'd kind of like all of us to do something like that together at the end of the play, but I don't know what."

"A play? I hadn't heard about this." Delight at their initiative tingled through Ruth.

The "director" beamed. "Sara and Clara wrote one together. It's about Queen Esther in the Bible."

"You did?" Ruth looked at the two girls. "That's terrific! Who is playing the men's parts?"

Both girls blushed, and June giggled. "They talked young Lionel and Michael into doing the King and Mordecai. When Phillip heard about it, he asked to be Haman."

Ruth groaned. "That sounds like Phillip. Is everybody in it?"

A chorus of agreement answered her.

"How have I not noticed what you were doing? I must have been totally unobservant."

"We kept it a secret deliberately," Sara hurried to reassure her. "We wanted to have it all planned before we told you so you wouldn't worry about it."

"Me? Worry?" Ruth tried to sound disbelieving. "Where are you getting the costumes?"

June turned pink this time. "Mrs. Spencer is showing me what to do with the scraps she, Ma, and Aunt Kate found for us."

"Do they know what's happening?"

"No." She shook her head emphatically. "At least Ma and Aunt Kate don't. We just told them we needed stuff for a surprise. I had to tell Mrs. Spencer so she could help me plan what everyone needs."

"You ladies amaze me." Ruth's students beamed under her praise. "Your initiative has made my day."

Six-year-old Audrey piped up. "What's 'nishutiv?"

"In this case, it's figuring out how to do something by yourself. You've shown initiative by making such a pretty picture without copying anyone else's." Ruth examined the youngster's drawing of a mass of brightly colored flowers. "Is everyone else finished?"

"Almost." "I will be in a minute." "As soon as I draw one more thing." The chorus indicated a unified conclusion.

Ruth remembered her only male student. "Where's Greg?"

"Here." The boy appeared in the doorway, his pockets sagging from their dense cargo and his hands holding a quart jar full of twigs, new grasses, and even a bit of moss. His shirt had come untucked from his pants, which showed evidence of close contact with mud, and his hair contained small bits of the same material he held in his jar. His eyes glowed with triumph. "It took me a long time," he explained unnecessarily, "but I found just the right stuff."

Ruth knew from experience how important "the right stuff" was to him. "What are you going to do now?"

He dumped his treasures on her desk. "Mom gave me this jar a long time ago, and I kept it in my fort for something special. See, if I turn it on its side like this, put the twigs in it like this and the moss like this, then the rocks look real nice on top. You'll have to be real careful, though." He looked at her with concern. "If you don't carry it right, it will get messed up."

She had to admit her brother had created an intriguing arrangement. It actually looked pretty, but she knew better than to say so. "I'll carry it properly and not let Sunset run while I'm taking it home."

"Do I still have to write sumthin'?" He looked at her hopefully.

"I would like you to at least make a note for Mrs. Pierce telling her who this is from and why you made it for her."

He wrinkled his forehead in thought. "I guess I can do that. As long as it doesn't have to be long."

Ruth shook her head with an indulgent smile. "First, though, I'd appreciate it if you'd clean off my desk and wash your hands. You don't want to get your paper smudged."

His expression didn't look as though he shared her concern, though he did follow instructions. While the girls tidied up after themselves and put the desks back in order, Greg sat hunched over his project. Finally, he looked up with an engaging grin. "Is this good enough, Ru—, I mean,

Miss McEvan?"

She stifled a grin of her own. Even after three years, her brothers still slipped up occasionally when addressing her. Dad had been the one to insist they call her "Miss McEvan" just like the rest of her students.

"Miss McEvan is your teacher, not your sister, when you're in that building. I don't want to hear of either of you trying to take advantage of her," he had informed them sternly at the beginning of each school year.

He won't have to make that speech this fall. She pushed aside the glum thought to examine Greg's work. The letters had obviously been formed carefully, in contrast to his usual scrawl. *"Dear Missus Pierce, I made this rock colekshun for you since Miss McEvan sed you was hurt. I hope you get well soon. Greg McEvan."*

"That's very nice," she approved. "Since everyone else is finished, shall we sit outside while I read another chapter in *Tom Sawyer*?"

A stampede for the door answered her suggestion. She rummaged on her desk for the book she'd begun reading aloud at the beginning of the year. Saved for special occasions, it looked like the story would last until the last day. She'd hoped to follow it with *The Adventures of Huckleberry Finn* next year.

Why does every day remind me of what I'll lose in just another six weeks? she wondered as she rode to the Pierces' two hours later with Greg's project carefully balanced in front of her. The students had gone home happy an hour ago, but she'd stayed to catch up on the never-ending quiz and composition papers. Her insides churned in turmoil. The school's closing still felt like a monumental loss. Her uncertain future now looked more complicated than ever.

She felt uneasy about accepting Jed's proposal. Yet a negative response would turn away what most likely would be her only chance to choose an alternative to spending the rest of her life as Timothy McEvan's old maid daughter. Unless, of course, she accepted Grandmother Carrington's offer.

She had started to guide Sunset toward the small pasture near the house when she noticed Sara sitting on the back porch. The girl didn't look upset, but Ruth felt a prickle of concern. Idleness simply didn't come naturally to Sara. "Is everything all right?" she called out, halting Sunset near the porch steps.

Sara's cheery smile reassured Ruth more than her words. "Perfectly. Mom's sleeping, so I didn't want to do anything noisy inside. You'd probably have time for a ride before she wakes up."

Tempted by the suggestion, Ruth felt compelled to protest. "What about supper?"

"Dad came in about half an hour ago and said we ought to plan for a late one and just let Mom sleep as long as she can. He said she hasn't rested well the last couple of nights."

"If you're sure—" Ruth still hesitated, not wanting to appear irresponsible.

"Go away." Sara's blue eyes twinkled as she waved a small hand toward the pasture. "If my brother were here, he'd say you need some time by yourself. I'll even take your things inside for you."

Uncanny perception must be a Pierce family trait, Ruth mused to herself as she handed over Greg's gift and her school satchel. A ride over some of the trails she and Theo had discovered together should at least quiet her tumultuous emotions enough to enable her to think clearly. She dismounted to open the gate into the pasture where the occupants of the former barn now grazed contentedly, led Sunset through, then fastened the gate back into place. Over in one corner a dark gray horse stood alone. The black splotch on his forehead exactly matched the color of his mane and tail. He turned his head toward the newcomers and nickered a greeting. As Sunset wandered toward the gray, thoughts of Theo came to the forefront of Ruth's mental tangle. Shadow, as Theo had named the horse, had taken the two of them on countless jaunts around the countryside. He and Sunset touched noses, and she leaned forward to stroke his head. Closing her eyes, she remembered the feel of galloping across a field, her arms wrapped around her friend, her cheek pressed against his back. The memory only intensified her futile wish to be able to talk everything over with him. She turned Sunset toward a trail that was just barely visible in the bush bordering the pasture. Aching for a long, hard gallop yet mindful of Dad's many warnings, she firmly held Sunset down to a walk. Neither she nor her horse knew this area well enough to hope to avoid the holes and low-lying soft spots that could cause a running animal to stumble. She'd never be able to forgive herself if her own carelessness hurt her horse.

On the other side of the bush line, the trail turned uphill, then flattened out at a small meadow. Ruth could see where the trail continued beyond this rise to another taller hill, but she turned back. The meadow provided an excellent view toward Pierces' farm and the schoolhouse just a bit to the northeast. She'd joined Theo and his family on many Sunday afternoon picnics at this spot. The landscape below had changed since her last visit here. Mr. Pierce had managed to clear another pasture area out of what had been a poplar stand, and one of his pastures had been plowed into a field. She smiled to herself, feeling quiet contentment that contrasted sharply with the day's emotional upheaval. She loved the way the farms and homesteads could alter the Peace River Country, yet leave it the same. She and Theo had often sat up here and discussed how the cycle of land development had a rhythm similar to the seasons, always predictable yet never identical. Both offered a reassuring sense of continuity. How had he endured six years of isolation from this world they both cherished? She tried to imagine seeing people instead of trees, houses instead of barns, well-tended yards instead of freshly plowed fields. According to Grandmother Carrington, Toronto offered the best in city living. Could it provide anything as satisfying as this view?

The question touched too closely to the thoughts she'd come here to escape. She nudged Sunset with her heels. "Let's go back, fellow. It's probably time to start working on supper."

Twilight had already begun to encroach on the evening by the time Ruth and Sara put the meal on the table. Mrs. Pierce apologized for sleeping so late, but her husband quickly reassured her. "You needed the rest, sweetheart. It hasn't hurt us a bit to wait a couple hours for supper."

Mrs. Pierce didn't look convinced, so Ruth added her own encouragement. "Besides, it gave me a chance to go exploring like Theo and I used to do. Remember that meadow where we used to go on family outings?"

Sara nodded. "It's been ages since we've been up there."

Teasing twinkles lit her dad's eyes. "You've appeared more interested in the view from Spencers' farm lately."

Sara blushed, but didn't lose her smile. "You're just jealous because I bake more cookies for Lionel than I do for you."

Mrs. Pierce grinned. "I think she has you there, dear."

"That's okay," Mr. Pierce replied. "I noticed Mrs. McEvan took pity on me and sent some of her jelly over. As long as you ladies keep me supplied with bread, I won't need cookies."

Now the teasing twinkles showed up in Sara's eyes as she stood to clear dishes from the table. "In that case, I'll just bring you a couple slices of bread for dessert, and the rest of us will enjoy the spice cake I made this afternoon."

"Why can't I have both?" He pretended to pout.

His wife patted his arm. "I'll give you part of my cake."

Ruth reveled in the banter, so much like her own family's antics. Mom often said humor made the difference between simply coping and actually enjoying life. Her ready laughter had been a welcome addition to the McEvan family after almost two years of unrelenting sadness. Now Ruth wondered if her first mother had laughed much. She'd been only twelve when the river had changed her life. Why couldn't she remember clearly anything before it?

"Mmm. That was well worth the wait. Thanks, girls." Mr. Pierce pushed back from the table and kissed his wife. "I have a couple more things to take care of before nightfall, so I'd better get back at it."

Mrs. Pierce sat in the dining room quietly looking outside while Ruth and Sara cleaned up after the meal. Sara had just let the last of the dirty dish water out of the kitchen sink when Ruth remembered her class project. "Did you give your mother her gifts?" she whispered.

Sara shook her head. "I thought you'd like to. I put them upstairs in your room."

Ruth ran upstairs to the pretty guest room and returned to the dining room with Greg's jar in one hand and the cards in the other. "My students wanted to let you know they were thinking about you this afternoon." She set the jar on the table in front of Mrs. Pierce, and laid the cards out side by side so her friend could look at them without having to pick them up. "Greg made this instead of a card, and the girls each made you a card."

With the edge of a bandage, Mrs. Pierce opened each card with damp-eyed delight. "How thoughtful of you to suggest they cheer me up! This is something your mother would have thought of. You're more like her all the time, you know."

Ruth paused in the doorway, afraid to voice the strange question that had come to mind. "Which mother?" she asked softly.

Her companion's gaze lifted from the pile of get well wishes. "I meant Ida, but now that I think of it, you're much like Janet, too."

"How well did you know my first mother?"

Mrs. Pierce stared out the window again, remembering. "I'd say we were friends. Why?"

Ruth forced her hands to stay busy wiping the already clean table. "I don't remember much about her anymore. I can't even recall things we used to do as a family before—" Her voice broke.

Mrs. Pierce let her collect herself before reminiscing in her gentle, cultured voice. "We didn't have long to become acquainted with your family before the tragedy happened, but since we were neighbors we helped each other quite a bit. My Doug helped your father clear the area where your house was built, and your dad helped clear our upper pasture in return. Janet was about your height with dark auburn hair. I guess you didn't have a chance at any other color with two red-headed parents." She coaxed a smile from Ruth with one of her own. "Her eyes sparkled with enthusiasm for everything and she never seemed to run out of energy. Most of all, she had a contagious love for God. She talked to Him and about Him like He was her best friend. I'm sure she's just as tickled about being in Heaven as she was with being alive down here."

The quiet words only increased Ruth's heartache. *Why would God have done such a terrible thing to someone who loved Him so much?* She dared not voice the thought. "I don't remember my brothers much, either. Even Daniel, my twin. I wish I had that much left of them."

Mrs. Pierce gestured with a bandaged hand toward the sitting room. "Please sit with me a moment. I'd like to tell you something I don't discuss much." Ruth obliged, and with pain-shadowed eyes the lady continued. "You've heard our family's story from Doug when he shared it with our fellowship group."

Ruth nodded, remembering the snowy Sunday at Spencers' farm. She'd cried for the first time since the river, and Ida had been there with tears of her own and hugs of comfort. It had marked the beginning of a kind of healing, though she still felt far from whole.

"Each baby who died took a piece of me. I thought their little faces would be imprinted in my memory forever. I struggled to imagine what they'd be like as they grew. The first time Sara called me 'Mama', I cried because I'd never heard it from my three babies. Doug let me weep for awhile, then ever so gently pointed out my grief was robbing me of the joy of Sara's important moments. I had to learn to release my little ones to the Heavenly Father whom they now know better than I did. While I can't tell you anymore what the babies looked like, I remember how their short lives brought me happiness." She smiled through tears. "If our memories remained vivid forever, our pain probably would, too, and that would be unbearable."

"Do you think she knows how we've felt and what's happened to us since she died?" Ruth whispered.

"Hebrews says we're surrounded by a cloud of witnesses made up of those believers who are already with God, so I think she does. She probably watches you even more closely than she did while she was here."

Ruth looked into the blue eyes in which compassion had replaced pain. "Why do you say that?"

"While she was alive, she loved you with a purely human love. Now she sees and understands you the way your Heavenly Father does and loves you just as much." She patted Ruth's leg softly with a bandaged hand.

The back door opened. "Cynthia, do you feel up to a walk?" Mr. Pierce called. "The sunset's really beautiful tonight."

Mrs. Pierce hurried to join her husband with the same delighted expression Mom wore when offered time alone with Dad. Ruth wandered up to her room feeling more unsettled than ever. She'd hoped happy memories of her mother would replace the horror-filled images that had plagued her at Grandma Lucy's. Instead, her quest had led her back to the nagging issue of her attitude toward God. If Mrs. Pierce were right, Mother knew Ruth wanted to keep God at a distance. She must be terribly disappointed. Yet if God had left well enough alone, Ruth wouldn't be questioning Him.

eleven

After nearly a week, Ruth had reached a decision. The more she'd thought about it, the less life with Grandmother Carrington appealed to her. At least if she married Jed, she'd be able to remain near those she loved and in a familiar, comfortable environment. Yet she felt in no hurry to communicate her decision to him. Whenever she saw him next would be soon enough.

As she explained in a letter to Theo, "*At least this way, my future is secured. Jed is a pleasant companion and I'm sure we can enjoy as many comfortable years together as life allows us. With a wedding to look forward to, the end of school won't seem so bleak.*" For the first time in their long friendship, she wondered if she was being completely honest with him.

Music practices were as successful as Ruth had hoped. The evening after the first one, Mr. Pierce met her at the edge of the pasture where she was saddling Sunset for an evening gallop. "Thanks for helping my wife. Bringing the girls over this afternoon lifted her spirits more than you can know."

She tugged on the saddle to ensure its straps were fastened securely and hurried to give due credit. "It was actually Sara's idea."

"But it wouldn't have happened without your encouragement." He stroked Sunset's pale mane. "How's the saddle working?"

"Perfectly." This was one subject about which Ruth could feel genuinely enthusiastic. "It's one of the nicest things anyone has ever done for me."

"You're more than worth it." He moved away from the fence. "Enjoy your ride."

She directed Sunset to the road before urging him to a full gallop. They thundered westward, past the turnoff toward home. Just before they reached the edge of Lars Harpers' freshly plowed land, she turned back. Tonight didn't feel like the right time to talk with Jed. With plenty of daylight still left, she decided to visit her favorite place by the creek and hoped her family wouldn't be offended that she'd been so close to home but hadn't stopped by. The water level had gone down quite a bit since her last visit. Its flow now seemed easy and peaceful. Too bad her life hadn't followed the same pattern. She began to fill another page in the book she'd left untouched since her last entry here at this very place.

> *I'm stretching*
> > *reaching for something I can't see.*
> *I don't know what's just beyond my fingertips*
> > *but I can almost touch it.*
> *There are some who see my helpless efforts,*
> > *who sense my restless spirit.*
> > *They know what's out there.*
> *Patiently, they watch me search, question, and*
> > *sometimes react.*
> > *They've already found.*
> *Why can't someone pass the secret on to me?*
> > *Why must I reach?*
> > *What will I grasp?*

They say trust is the key
  But I don't understand.
How can I depend on something which makes
  no sense?
Maybe someday I'll see it, touch it, claim it for
  my own.
I can always hope.

With her future at least partially arranged, she found school less heart-wrenching than usual. Remembering what Mrs. Pierce had said, she made a point of enjoying each day in the classroom as much as possible. The throbbing ache in her heart had disappeared, replaced by a kind of emptiness. Even questions about trusting God didn't plague her so much. Yet something Grandma Lucy had said wouldn't leave her alone. "You're trying to control your life so well you don't have to depend on Him. God will let you run things on your own until you realize how puny your understanding is compared to His wisdom. When you get desperate enough, you'll discover how easy it is to trust."

Ten days after the fire, she moved back home. Mrs. Pierce had held her in a long embrace as Ruth had prepared to leave. "Thanks for coming," she'd whispered. "You're a treasure."

Ruth wished she felt like a treasure instead of a bundle of confusion. She'd thought making a decision about Jed would unravel her feelings. Perhaps telling him what she'd decided would help.

Her entire family met her in the barn with hugs and exclamations of welcome. "Don't go 'way, never 'gen," Beth instructed, wagging her chubby baby fingers.

Mom laughed. "She's asked about you every day. I finally had to ask Greg not to talk about school when she could hear. You should have seen the tantrum when she discovered he saw you every day and she couldn't. Then I had to keep her and Timmy home Sunday because they had the sniffles. I was not the world's most popular mother."

"I've missed you guys, too." She revelled in their welcoming affection. "Greg, would you ride over to Jed's for me and ask him if he can come over tonight?"

Dad's bushy eyebrows lifted. "You're not in a hurry to see him, are you?"

Ruth felt a flush stain her cheeks. "The night of the fire, he asked me to marry him. I still haven't given him my answer."

Her parents waited until Greg had gone and Phillip had disappeared to his fort before pursuing the subject. "So are you going to let us in on the secret or keep us in suspense?" Dad inquired as they sat around the table enjoying cups of tea. Mom's knitting dropped to her lap as she watched her daughter intently.

The question made Ruth uncomfortable, but there was no reason not to answer. "I'm going to tell Jed yes."

A shadow passed over Mom's face. "Are you sure about this, honey?"

Ruth felt sure she'd chosen her only real option. "Yes. He treats me with respect and will be a good provider." Even to her ears, the words sounded defensive.

Dad studied the tabletop before looking up with a false smile. "Congratulations! Have you set a date?"

Apprehension briefly knotted Ruth's middle. Choosing a wedding date would move her decision from the realm of contemplation to reality. For the first time, she realized she was about to make a commitment that would change her life. "We'll probably discuss it tonight."

Mom laid her handwork aside. "I'll go get the little ones into bed, then whip up a cake so we can celebrate."

Dad and Ruth sat in uneasy silence. She'd never felt restraint with him before. When their gazes finally met, she saw her uncertainty reflected in his eyes. He reached out for her hand and cleared his throat. "You don't have to do this, Ruthie."

"I know." She tried to speak with conviction. "I'm doing it because I want to."

"But why?" He seemed to search her inner thoughts. "I don't think you love Jed. That won't make for an easy marriage."

She shrugged. "Love will come as we live and work together."

He cleared his throat again. "Ever since you and Daniel were born, I've dreamed of the day when you'd look at some wonderful young man the way your mother looked at me on our wedding day. Why don't you wait until you know you love him?"

"Because I don't want to." She knew her words would hurt him, but if she didn't make him understand, he'd talk her out of her tenuous decision. "I don't want to feel about anyone the way you and Mother felt about each other. If something happens to Jed, I want to be able to go on. Jed isn't madly in love with me, either, so it's not like I'll be taking advantage of him. Besides, if I don't marry him, who else is there?"

Pain filled Dad's eyes, though it seemed to be more for her than for himself. "You're short-changing yourself, little girl." Hoofbeats in the yard caught his attention. He gave her hands a final squeeze. "I just want to see you happy."

"I will be." She stood. "It's plenty light out, so we'll probably wander around outside for awhile, but I'll make sure Jed comes in before he leaves."

To her intense relief, Jed didn't try to kiss her when she gave him her news. He just enfolded her hand in his large, calloused one. "You've made me very pleased."

She let him hold her hand for awhile before tugging it loose to point at a nest near the top of a tall pine. "Do you have any idea what kind of bird is building up there?"

He squinted upward for a moment. "Can't say I do. It's probably not good for eating or dangerous to the stock, so I don't pay much attention."

Ruth's parents had encouraged her to find out as much as she could about the plants and creatures with whom they shared the land. They'd praised curiosity and tried to help her find answers. "Don't you ever want to know about something just for the fun of finding out?"

Bafflement spread across his face. "Learnin' never was much fun for me. If it don't help me run the farm better, I don't need it clutterin' up my head."

What a boring way to live, Ruth thought, but kept it to herself. This man would become her husband. She had to learn to accept his way of thinking even if it differed from her own. "When do you think we ought to get married? Dad and Mom were asking if we'd set a date."

"It depends on whether you're set on takin' a trip." His tone, though pleasant enough, indicated he didn't feel much enthusiasm for the idea. "We'd have to wait until after harvest in that case."

She wanted to be settled into her new home by the time school started again. "Then we'd be travelling in snow and cold. I don't think we need a trip."

"Then let's get married near the end of June. The first hay crop won't be ready to come off until mid-July."

"Shall we go in and look at Mom's calendar?"

He nodded approval and reached for her hand again. She didn't pull away. Dad and Mom would notice if there weren't some show of affection.

Whatever their reservations, they welcomed Jed enthusiastically. Dad shook his hand and thumped his back. "Welcome to the family, son."

Jed's blush deepened when Mom hugged him. "You'd better get used to it," she teased. "I don't plan to treat a son-in-law any different from my other sons. Hugs are routine around here."

Phillip and Greg appeared from their room to see what the fuss was all about. "Ruth and Jed are getting married," Dad informed them.

"When?" Greg looked uncertain.

"We actually came in looking for a calendar so we can decide just that." Ruth looked at the page tacked up on the kitchen wall. "What about June 27th? That will give me two weeks to get ready after school is out."

Mom pulled a pan from the oven. "Come sit, everybody. Who wants coffee and who wants tea?"

Greg and Phillip both asked for coffee along with Jed and Dad, and were actually given some. Mom and Ruth sipped tea. "Do you know yet where you're going to live?" Mom asked.

"Pa's given me a few acres just across the creek. We'll probably stay in the big house until I can get a cabin built. Ma's really lookin' forward to having Ruth around."

Ruth avoided looking at her mother, their previous

conversations about Kate Harper replaying in her memory. Could she handle sharing a house with the incessant talker?

"May I have the honor of announcing your plans this Sunday?" Dad asked. "If you don't mind, I'll see if we can get a cabin-raising organized for the weekend before the wedding. You young folks ought to have a place of your own from the start."

Jed shifted uncomfortably, his ears reddening. "I'd rather not be beholden. This is a busy season for everyone."

"Then perhaps you ought to postpone the wedding." Dad spoke conversationally, but Ruth heard a subtle challenge. "Adjusting to marriage is challenge enough without having to continue living with one set of parents or the other."

Evidently, Jed heard it, too. He met Dad's gaze directly. "I guess folks wouldn't come if they didn't want to."

A smile softened Dad's expression. "Just like you wouldn't have helped fight the fire if you hadn't wanted to. We all need each other from time to time. That's what pioneering's all about."

Dad's announcement on Sunday brought cheers and applause. Every man present promised to help with the cabin raising, and Mr. Albertson offered to supply windows "as our wedding gift to the kids."

Kate Harper hurried over to Ruth with a beaming smile. "I'm so proud I could burst," she exclaimed unnecessarily. "My Jed's one of the most responsible men in the Peace River Country, and you're the finest young woman I know. It will be wonderful having you as neighbors just across the creek. You're sure you don't want to get married a little sooner?"

"Don't be rushing them, Kate," Nina Spencer intervened. "Ruth has a school year to finish first."

"Didn't this work out fine?" Mrs. Harper's enthusiasm continued unabated as she and Mrs. Spencer approached the food-laden table together, her voice carrying well. "I was beginnin' to wonder if she'd ever get married, bein' so attached to her teachin'. Not that it wasn't good for our children to have such a devoted teacher, but gettin' married and havin' babies is what girls her age are meant to do. Most girls settle even younger. Take my Nettie, for instance. Why, she was only 16 when she and Jeff married. Little Aaron will be four by the time she's Ruth's age. Did I tell you he's already—"

"I hope you don't mind my mother." Jed approached with two laden plates. "Since she kinda had you cornered, I took the liberty of getting you some dinner."

"Thank you. That's very thoughtful." Ruth's smile came from her heart. If today was any indication, coping with her future mother-in-law would not be easy. Her suspicion strengthened into conviction a week later.

Mrs. Harper sent Teddy to the schoolhouse with a message for Ruth on Friday afternoon. "Ma says to ask you to come for dinner tomorrow night, and to come as early in the afternoon as you want."

Ruth saddled Sunset shortly after four Saturday afternoon. Though she felt nervous about time alone with Mrs. Harper, she didn't want to insult the lady by not accepting the invitation to come early. This way, they'd only have an hour or two before the men came home from the fields.

Mrs. Harper seemed to have been watching for her. "Just take your horse to the corral and leave your saddle on the fence. The men will take care of it later," she called from the door.

Ruth followed instructions, though she felt uncomfortable about it. "If you can use something," Dad always said, "you can put it away properly." Dumping her saddle on the fence rail certainly didn't fit that description, but neither could she simply hang it anywhere in the barn. Sunset certainly needed to be brushed down after the ride, but it also seemed rude to help herself to the Harpers' tools. She patted his neck. "I hate to do this to you, old pal, but I don't have a choice. I'll make it up to you when we get home."

Mrs. Harper met her in the yard. "I was hoping you'd be able to make it early, but I know how busy you must be with school and helping your ma and all. How is she feeling? The first few months are always so hard when one's in the family way. My Nettie thought she'd die. She and Jeff will be here in about an hour. That'll give you and me a chance for a real good visit. Now just sit there at the table and relax while I finish this cake I've planned for dessert. Jed loves spice cake. I'll have to be sure to give you all his favorite recipes, though I hope you two will feel free to just pop over here for a meal anytime you like. I envy you, being able to start your marriage so close to family. Lars and I moved out here right after our wedding so I had to learn everything by myself. He's an easy man to please, my Lars is, and Jed's pretty much the same." She poured the batter into a pan and placed it in the oven.

Sitting across the table from Ruth, she continued. "Did I ever tell you how Lars and I met? His family moved to the prairies from Norway when Lars was 13 and James, 10. The boys had to work just like men right from the start, so neither finished school. Lars knew hardly any English when I met him. My parents had also come from Norway when they were children, so I'd learned enough Norwegian from them to help Lars learn English. He was 21 and I was 16 when we married in a double ceremony with James and Ruby. Then the four of us moved out here. We started on a single homestead in Lars' name, then two years later James and Ruby started over on their own land. They got their lean-to finished just two weeks before James Jr. was born. I'll never know why they had to go and have seven children. I mean, your folks have six, but that's two families. No one expected Ida not to have babies just because your dad already had you three."

Ruth involuntarily thought of the days when her other brothers had been alive, then moved her thoughts to the six Spencer children. Large families were more common around here than small ones, but she wasn't given an opportunity to volunteer her opinion.

"Let me show you around our house real quick before I have to get dinner on the table. The men should be back soon."

Ruth followed her future mother-in-law throughout the two-story house, murmuring appropriate admiration when they reached the parlor.

"When Lars decided to build us a regular house to replace our old cabin seven years ago, I told him I wanted a parlor. He thought it a foolish idea, but built it anyway. Our bedroom is here at the back, and the children's bedrooms are upstairs. Of course, Nettie's is empty now, and Jed's will be at the end of next month." She smirked sideways at Ruth. "But it won't be long before we'll have grandchildren all over the place, and the rooms will be put to good use."

Ruth willed the heat out of her cheeks, wishing Mrs. Harper wouldn't be so plain-spoken. She didn't want to think about having children just yet.

But her thoughts took a completely different direction when Nettie and Jeff arrived, bearing baby Aaron. "Let Miss McEvan hold him," Nettie instructed her husband, a short, blond young man with friendly brown eyes.

"I think since we're going to be sisters, you might as well call me Ruth," the former teacher requested, holding out her arms for Jeff's tiny burden.

"It may take me awhile to get used to being so familiar-like, but I'm real glad we're going to be family. If you don't mind keeping watch on the baby, I'll help Ma. There's Pa and the boys coming now, Jeff. They'll be glad of a hand with chores." Nettie obviously had not lost her childhood powers of organization.

Ruth sat with her back to the table, silently savoring Aaron's weight in her arms. She'd loved holding Timmy and Beth when they were tiny, but this felt different. What would it be like to hold a child of her own? He lay sleeping, a perfect picture of peace, totally undisturbed by the chatter and clatter created by his mother and grandmother. The vague desire she'd carried for months abruptly became full-fledged yearning. She fervently hoped she wouldn't have to wait long for her own baby.

He awakened just before the men came inside, so Nettie hustled him off for a feeding. "Go ahead and start without me," she instructed her mother. "I'll join you after Aaron's finished."

To Ruth's relief, the men had plenty to discuss as the food dishes passed from hand to hand around the table. Who knew what Mrs. Harper would say if talk moved to more general matters? She didn't have to wait long to find out.

"I'm sure Ruth's not interested in dirt and weather." She looked at Jeff. "I don't guess we've formally introduced you two. This is Ruth McEvan, one of Nettie's former teachers and Jed's fiancèe. They'll be getting married at the end of next month."

"Congratulations," Jeff commented politely. "Will you be buying land nearby?"

Mrs. Harper didn't give Jed or Ruth a chance to answer for themselves. "Oh, no. They'll be building just on the other side of the creek so Jed can continue helping his Pa on the farm."

Teddy used his fork to stab a piece of bread in the basket near the center of the table and lift it to his plate while grinning mischievously at Ruth. "You'll have a longer walk to school next year."

"She won't teach after she gets married," his mother informed him, "and ask for things to be passed. Ruth will think we've raised you in the barn."

From her experiences with the boy in school, Ruth recognized the glint in his eyes. He'd reached across the table just to get a reaction from his mother. She squelched the urge to wink at him.

"What's this I hear about consolidation?" Jeff asked, passing the mashed potatoes to his wife, who'd just sat down. "I haven't gone to any of the meetings since everything will probably change again before Aaron gets to school."

Mr. Harper explained what he knew of the plan from his role as trustee. *If Mrs. Harper hadn't just put a piece of pork roast in her mouth, she probably would have answered,* Ruth thought uncharitably. Her hostess' comment had struck a tender spot that still hadn't quit throbbing when Jed helped Ruth saddle Sunset for the ride home.

"Thanks for coming," he said. "Ma was real happy to have you over."

Ruth hid her feelings behind a smile. "It was nice to meet Jeff. I'll see you tomorrow?"

"Maybe I'll ride my black to the service and we can go for a ride together after lunch." He appeared eager to do something that would please her.

"That will be fun." She nudged Sunset with her heel. "Good night."

He opened the corral gate and waved her out.

Her future mother-in-law's comments continued to rankle while Ruth rode home. It felt as though she would be expected to meld into the family without even a ripple of independence. Mrs. Harper even seemed to think Jed and Ruth would be a mere extension of her household rather than a new family on their own. For the first time since accepting Jed's proposal, Ruth allowed herself to wonder if she'd decided wisely.

twelve

Two weeks later, on a Tuesday afternoon, Dad stopped by the schoolhouse. "Had to go to town for a new bridle for Star, and picked up the mail. I thought maybe you'd like to read this here." He held out an envelope addressed in Theo's writing.

The tension in Ruth's shoulders eased a little. "Thanks."

"Have you told him about Jed?"

"I sent a letter to him the day after I decided."

"Does Jed know about your correspondence?"

Her gaze met his in surprise. "Does it matter?"

He lowered himself to one of the desktops. "Maybe not to Jed. Personally, I wouldn't take too kindly to your mom writing regularly to another man."

"But Theo's my best friend!"

"He has been a good friend," Dad agreed gently. "That will have to change, though, honey. You and Jed are preparing to commit yourselves to each other for life. If any man is your best friend, it should be your husband."

Ruth tried to imagine telling Jed some of the things she wrote to Theo. "Jed's not that kind of person."

Pain flickered in Dad's face. "Then maybe you should reconsider about marrying him."

His words resembled the feelings Ruth had been trying to ignore. "I can't do that, Dad. I gave him my word. Besides, people have already started giving us stuff, and the cabin raising is already scheduled."

"Ruthie, please listen to me." His voice deepened to a rumble and he waited for her to look into his eyes. "There is absolutely no valid reason for you to marry Jed unless you want to. You can return gifts. The cabin building can be cancelled. Once you say 'I do,' you're in it for life. After that, you can only make the best of what you have. Until June 27, however, you are free to change your mind. It's better for both you and Jed to suffer a little embarrassment now rather than spend a lifetime together in a marriage you're not happy in. If you're not happy, he won't be either."

She felt entangled in a web of her own making from which there seemed to be no escape. "I don't know what I should do anymore."

"Have you asked your Heavenly Father about it?"

How could she tell him how she felt about God? "I think I'm too scrambled to pray coherently."

"God doesn't care how fancy we talk. He only wants to know that we want what He knows is best for us. If we're willing to listen, He's willing to show us the way."

"Then ask Him to show me what's right," Ruth whispered, afraid she'd start to cry.

Dad hugged her against himself, his shirt smelling like dirt, sweat, and horses. "My wonderful daughter, your mom and I bring you before the Lord first thing every morning and last thing every night. We won't stop even after you're married. Please don't be afraid to talk with us if we can help."

She enjoyed the secure feeling of resting against his muscled strength. "You're pretty wonderful yourself."

He pulled back with a grin. "Your brothers aren't going

to think I'm so wonderful when I return and put them back
to work. I'll see you tonight."

Long after the clump of his boots faded away, she sat
staring at Theo's unopened letter. Dad was right. As much
as it hurt to consider, her friendship with Theo would have
to develop distance if she went through with marrying Jed.
If she broke her engagement, she and Theo could stay
friends, but only until he married. Then she'd be left without a husband, a job, or a friend. She slowly slit the edge
of the envelope, savoring what would probably be her last
letter from him.

> *My dear friend,*
>
> *I read your latest letter with more concern
> than joy. You didn't write like someone
> preparing to share her life with a man she
> loves. I wish I could be there to look into
> your face and see that my fears are ground-
> less.*
>
> *I hope I'm not out of line to encourage
> you to pray carefully about your upcoming
> marriage. Make sure you're making the
> wisest decision, not just grasping at straws
> because your future looks uncertain. No one
> who matters will blame you for changing
> your mind if you need to. Even though Jed
> would probably be hurt, if he's the man I
> think he is he'd rather have you back out
> now than make a mistake which will affect
> his life as much as yours.*
>
> *My future is looking rather uncertain, as*

*well. Plans had almost been finalized for me
to return to the Peace area and set up my
practice. However, something has come up
which will delay those plans, if not change
them altogether.*

*This will probably be my last letter to you.
Though I'll always consider you my very
dear friend, continuing our correspondence
wouldn't be doing right by Jed. I'll miss your
letters and continue to pray for you with all
my heart.*

*Please tell Jed I congratulate him on his
choice of a fine wife. I hope the two of you
will be very happy.*

Tears streamed down her cheeks as she returned the letter to its envelope. Her heart felt torn out by the roots. Theo's friendship had been her strength for more than ten years, even during those horrible grief-blackened days that still haunted her. She thought she'd endured the ultimate in pain then, but she knew now how wrong she'd been. At least she'd had Theo to lean on. She had to face this alone. She felt utterly abandoned.

By the time she walked home, her tears had dried into quiet agony. Dad must have told Mom about their discussion because she said nothing about Ruth's reddened eyes, or her request to remain in her room while the family ate supper. Not only had her appetite vanished, but she couldn't bear either kindness or curiosity from anyone just now. Besides, she had to pull herself together. Jed would arrive in just a couple of hours. She either had to mask her feelings or explain them to him. Lying face down on her bed, she dozed fitfully. At the last minute, she forced herself upright, returned her hair to tidiness, and pasted a smile on her lips as she pulled on her long riding skirt. She'd ride to meet Jed. If she had to visit with him under her parents' knowing glances, her hard-won composure would shatter.

Jed's face lit with a delighted smile when he saw her. "This is a pleasant surprise. How was your day?"

"Not bad," she murmured. "How was yours?"

"We're almost finished seeding, and three different buyers stopped by to look at horses. One of them is interested in my colt out of the sorrel mare by my black. He offered an incredible price if I'll have him broken to bridle by fall." If he noticed her lack of response, he didn't comment.

They continued riding west in silence for several miles. On impulse, Ruth urged Sunset into a gallop. Rather than holding him back as she usually did when riding with Jed, she let him go. Jed's black kept up for awhile, but Sunset gradually began to pull away. It made Ruth feel as if she had shed his mother's confining expectations, the heartache of Theo's letter, the burden of trying to force herself to feel the way a bride-to-be ought to feel. Sunset's labored breathing finally caught her attention. She reined him down to a trot.

"What was that for? If I didn't know better, I'd think you was tryin' to make me and my black look bad."

Jed's faintly accusing voice made her turn Sunset to face him. Veiled hurt showed in his eyes. His black was their prize stud. Though she'd sensed for awhile that Sunset could outrun the black, she hadn't known for sure. As a horse breeder, his horse's superior speed was part of his professional reputation.

"I'm sorry." She gulped down the urge to correct his colloquial grammar, which only reminded her of Theo's precise speech and wide vocabulary. "I didn't realize. . . I didn't know. . ." Her voice trailed off.

"Just don't tell anyone. I can't have folks knowin' my wife's horse is better than mine."

"I'm not your wife." The unwise words shot from her mouth before she could stop them.

"You will be, unless of course you're thinkin' of changin' your mind."

She plucked at Sunset's mane, unwilling to reveal her doubts but unable to reassure him.

"C'mon, Ruth." He slid from his horse and held out his arms to her. "We can't talk like this. Come down and we'll walk for awhile. The horses could use the rest, anyway."

Dismounting without his assistance, she ignored the subtle accusation. She wrapped the reins around both hands.

Jed noticed. "What is it? I don't think it's such a bad thing for me to want to touch you. We're engaged, so we should be gettin' used to each other."

His words intensified her guilt. If she really loved him, she'd welcome his touch. If she didn't love him, why was she pursuing this sham? How long before he saw through her act?

"Ruth, please talk to me. I know something's not right. Since the Saturday after our engagement, you've refused to visit our farm again. Sunday's the only chance my ma has to get to know you, but you avoid her. I know she's not the easiest person to visit with, but you have to get used to her pretty soon. She'll be your closest friend durin' most of the summer. You're going to be too busy helpin' her to go ridin' off elsewhere, and me and Pa are goin' to be busy from dawn till dark."

Ruth couldn't stop tears of frustration. "That's just the point. You and your ma both assume because I'm marrying you I'm going to become just another Harper. She's mentioned several times how blessed I must feel to be marrying you rather than having to find another job. Why can't I be married to you and a teacher, too? What's wrong with that?"

He looked puzzled. "But I thought you said awhile back you wouldn't be able to find another school."

"Even if I could, though, your ma wouldn't want me to take it."

"I wouldn't either, but it's not a question. So why fret about it?" His voice remained deliberately calm.

She stopped walking and looked directly into his face. "Can't you see that *is* the question? You're not paying any attention to the kind of person I am inside. Learning and teaching have been my life for seventeen years. Why must I abandon it simply because I'm marrying you?"

"But your school is closing, so it doesn't matter."

"Yes, it does, Jed." Frustration sharpened her voice. "You don't know there's any life beyond your fields and your horses. I'm not like that. I'm curious about the outside world. I like to learn and to teach. I have to have more than endless days of cleaning, gardening, and cooking."

He shrugged. "I s'pose we could subscribe to the town paper, if you like, and Ma'll be glad to teach you to knit."

She couldn't decide whether to laugh or cry. "You can't

understand, can you? It's not what I do that matters. It's the kind of person I am."

"But Ma really likes you. In a few months, you'll get used to us."

Maybe he'd understand if she explained her feelings differently. "Jed, you told me a bit ago I couldn't tell anyone Sunset's faster than your black. That doesn't make any more sense to me than my teaching does to you. Why does it matter if my horse can run faster?"

Embarrassment tinged his face. "Because you're my wife, or will be next month," he quickly amended.

His reply stung. "And what difference does that make?"

"Can't you see it, Ruth? If another man breeds a better horse, that's business. If a woman breeds a better horse, that's business. But for my wife to ride a better horse, I'll be a laughingstock! I won't take him back. Since he's gelded, he wouldn't be much practical use to me anyway. Just, please, don't let on he's faster than my black."

"You've forgotten an important point about Sunset." Ruth fought back hysteria. Jed's attitude on the heels of Theo's letter had stretched her nerves almost to the breaking point. "My parents bought him as my birthday present. When, or if, I become your wife, Sunset remains mine. Do you hear that? Mine! I may have to give away part of myself to marry you, but I'm not handing over my horse."

"I still don't understand." Jed looked more betrayed than hurt.

She swallowed hard to calm herself. "Jed, do you realize how different I am from your mother and sister? I could become fond of your ma, but I'm not ready to let her or you run my life."

"Then perhaps you shouldn't be marrying me."

His inability to see her perspective had pushed her past the point of caring about his feelings. "Perhaps I shouldn't."

"I'd like to change your mind, Ruth." He looked at her with sad brown eyes. "But I don't want you to become my wife because you feel you have to. I'll ride with you back to your farm, but I won't come to see you again unless you ask. If you haven't sent a message to me by Sunday, I'll call off the wedding."

Ruth turned her back to him. "Please just leave me alone. I'll make it back by myself."

"If that's the way you want it." His black's hoofbeats made the only sound as he rode away.

She wrapped her arms around her horse's neck and buried her face in his mane. "What have I done, Sunset? I'm so confused I don't know anything anymore." A fresh torrent of tears dimmed her eyes as she hoisted herself into the saddle. "I can't become the kind of wife they expect. But in another month, I won't be a teacher anymore. I have nothing left." Scarcely noticing where Sunset took her, she let weeping take over. She rode and cried until exhausted. Should she write Theo about what had happened? If she didn't write back, she wouldn't have to endure the pain of breaking off their letters when he married. She didn't think she could endure this afternoon's grief again.

Her thoughts drifted back to the evening Justin had abandoned her in town. Jed now probably felt similar to the way she'd felt that night that seemed so long ago. Her fierce independence had hurt them both. What if she had chosen trust as Grandma Lucy had suggested?

"God, I'm tired," she found herself praying. "I don't know what You would have had me do differently, but I wish I'd tried to listen to You. I don't know if You're even listening to me anymore. You obviously aren't going to tell me why You let my family drown. Will You at least make sense out of the mess I've created? If it's not too late for me to learn, I want to find out how to trust You." The tears that flowed this time finally brought release.

Dusk had begun to fall when she finally took stock of her surroundings. They'd wandered off the road into a pasture she thought might belong to Doug Pierce. At least she hoped so. She'd hate to be caught trespassing on someone else's land. If she didn't return home soon, Dad would worry. Her heels prodded Sunset into his long, easy gallop. She glimpsed the Pierces' home off to the left, which meant the road should be not far ahead. How they'd wandered so far, she couldn't explain. Her head hurt. Leaning low over Sunset's neck, she closed her gritty eyes. He stumbled once, then twice. She only had time to wish she'd heeded Dad's warning not to gallop in unfamiliar fields before she felt her body launched into the air.

thirteen

Ruth squinted her eyes open. Judging by the sunlight streaming painfully around the edge of the curtain, she figured she must have overslept drastically. She tried to sit up and swing her legs over the side of her bed, but pain knifed through her left leg as gentle hands pushed her shoulders back onto the pillow. "Quiet, Ruth. Don't try to move."

The voice sounded like Grandma Lucy's. What was she doing here? Why did she hurt all over? She tried to remember. *Theo's letter.* Grief clogged her throat again, though it didn't explain why she was trapped here in bed. Her leg remained immovable.

"What happened?" Her voice sounded croaky. She tried to focus bleary eyes.

"You've broken your leg and have a nasty bump on your head. Dr. Watson says you're not to get up for at least another day. He'll be by this afternoon."

"How? What about school?" More questions than answers flooded her mind. Why couldn't she remember?

"Your mother's taken your classes. Just rest." Grandma placed a cool cloth on her head.

Ruth pushed it away. "No. I have to know what happened. I can't remember."

Grandma's smile brought no reassurance. "I'll get your dad. He's the one who found you." She left the room quietly.

Found her? Where had she been? The pain in her body

143

felt insignificant compared to her hurting emotions. Why did she feel so awful?

"I hear you're awake." Dad's face slowly came into focus. He looked like he'd been up all night. Something sad hid in his eyes.

"I think so." Ruth reached for his hand and tried to smile. "If I'm dreaming, I hope I wake up soon. I hurt all over."

He lowered himself onto the bed. "You and Sunset fell."

She remembered crying into Sunset's mane. "Where? Why?"

"I don't know why you were in Pierces' pasture. We just found you there early this morning."

Pierces' pasture. She recalled seeing their house off to the left. In a horrible rush, it all came back. She and Jed had argued. She'd told him she couldn't marry him. Sunset had stumbled. "Sunset?"

Dad's eyes told her wordlessly.

She tried to turn away, to bury her sobs in her pillow, but the weight on her leg kept her helplessly in place. "It was my fault. I didn't mean to, but I wanted to come home. I killed him." Though it hurt to cry, it hurt more to try to stifle it.

Dad lay down beside her and cradled her head against his shoulder. "It's all right, Ruthie. Hush, honey. It's all right, little girl." His endearments continued until her sobs quieted.

Her head ached too much to think anymore. Nestled in his comforting embrace, she let sleep claim her again.

Dad still lay beside her when she awoke. He lifted himself up to look down into her face. "How're you doin'?"

Her memory hadn't faded this time. Tears filled her eyes again, but Dad's comforting presence made the sorrow bearable. "Awful."

"Do you feel like talking?"

Her attempted nod set off drumbeats in her head.

"Jed stopped by to tell us the wedding is off." He searched her eyes for a reaction.

"He didn't tell you it was my fault?"

Dad traced her cheeks tenderly with calloused fingers, wiping away tears. "No. He just said he wanted us to know where you were and that you'd asked to be alone."

"I can't marry him."

"I know, Ruthie. I'm just glad you found out before it's too late."

"Sunset—" As soon as she said his name, she remembered. "He's dead."

Dad's hand cupped her cheek comfortingly. "His leg broke when he fell. I'm sorry."

"It's my fault. You told me not to let him run except on the road. You gave him to me and I killed him." Weeping took over once more.

"Ruth!" Dad's voice sharpened. He shook her shoulder. Her throbbing head halted the hysteria.

"Ruth, listen to me." Absolute authority replaced tender sympathy in his voice. He lowered his head so she had no place to look but directly into his eyes. "We know you made a mistake last night. Sunset paid part of the price, and you're paying for it with a headache, a broken leg, and a hurting heart. But Ruthie," his voice softened, "we still love you. Sunset was just a horse. We can't afford to replace him right away; however, as soon as we can, we will."

Shutting her eyes against the pain, she whispered, "I don't want another horse."

"Get her to drink this," Grandma's voice suggested.

Ruth felt her head and shoulders being lifted by Dad's muscled arm and a cool glass pressed against her mouth. "Please drink, honey," he softly commanded. With her eyes still shut, she obeyed. It was an unfamiliar taste, but soothing. Welcome blackness enfolded her.

The next time she woke up, the sunlight didn't seem nearly as bright. Her head still hurt. "Dad? Grandma?" She felt Grandma's soothing presence even before the beloved face leaned over her.

"Right here, child."

"Where's Dad?"

"He's in the fields today. If you need him, I only have to blow the whistle he left." She gently brushed Ruth's tangled curls back from her face.

"Today? But he was here when I went to sleep." Her mind still refused to function clearly.

Grandma laughed gently. "That was yesterday afternoon, dear one."

"Who's taking care of your boardinghouse?"

"Nina, and before you ask, Clara's plenty big enough to cook for her family while Nina's helping me. Anything else you want to worry about?" she teased.

Ruth didn't feel like smiling. "So many people... messed up... because of me." She had to swallow hard between each phrase.

"Now that's enough of that, young lady." Grandma spoke sternly. "Self-pity is not allowed in my presence. I'm here because I love you, Nina's where she is because she loves both of us, and the change is good preparation for Clara. Can you remember my verse?"

It took a moment, but the words gradually filtered into

her memory, bringing profound reassurance. "The steps of a good woman are ordered by the Lord." She lay silently, savoring the peace. Why did it feel so newly familiar? Something had happened before she had fallen, even before she'd foolishly urged her horse to run. Pushing back guilt, she forced herself to remember each detail. "Grandma?"

"Yes?" She hadn't left Ruth's side.

"I remembered something good about last night." She corrected herself. "Or I guess it was night before last, since I slept all day yesterday."

"You needed it," Grandma soothed. "What's the happy memory?"

"I asked God to teach me to trust." The simple words caused unbelievable peace to seep into her spirit.

Grandma's reply was barely above a whisper. "I'm so glad, child. It looks like He's given you plenty of time to practice."

Denial rose abruptly to her lips. Her present situation resulted only from her own stubborn choices. "This has nothing to do with Him."

"Nonsense. He didn't quit being God just because you were ignoring Him."

"How did you know I was ignoring Him?"

Grandma chuckled. "How do you know when your brother is upset with your dad? When you love two people, you just know."

"I still don't know why Mother and the boys had to drown." Even as she spoke, the answer didn't seem nearly as important as it had.

"And you probably never will know." Grandma sat beside her and stroked the back of her hand. "'Why' is one question God often leaves unanswered. I like to believe its answer is simply too complex for our finite minds. We just aren't capable of seeing from God's perspective yet. Until we can, we have to leave the question with Him."

Ruth felt sleep creeping up on her again, but she fought to finish the conversation. "It used to be too hard."

"God's wonderful that way. Sometimes all we have to do is let Him know we're willing, and He does the rest. Go ahead and sleep now. It's the best thing for you. I'll still be here when you're ready to talk again."

By the third day, Ruth's body no longer demanded endless hours of sleep. "I'm already awake," she announced when Grandma tiptoed through the door, then laughed at the lady's startled expression.

"My, aren't we chipper?" Grandma's eyes crinkled with the affectionate smile that always made Ruth feel uniquely loved.

"I doubt I'm ready to go rock picking, but my head doesn't feel like a woodpecker lives inside anymore."

"In that case, how would you like a sponge bath and a hair wash?"

It sounded heavenly. "Could we really?"

"Absolutely. A clean body always feels healthier than a dirty one. But first, do you mind if the little ones come in to say hi? They've been fretting themselves sick because we wouldn't let them in here."

"Sure." She suddenly realized how long it had been since she'd seen any of her family other than Dad. Remembering his comforting presence filled her eyes again. "I'll see if I can keep from crying for a few minutes."

"Don't fight it, child." Grandma patted Ruth's shoulder. "You've been through a lot emotionally and physically.

Tears are God's way of helping us cope."

Her kindness caused Ruth's eyes to overflow. With a lacy, sweet-smelling hanky, Grandma dried Ruth's cheeks. "Now," she announced briskly when the shower had passed. "Let's prop you up on a couple of pillows and bring the babies in."

Ruth heard Beth's squeal and Timmy's running footsteps before Grandma even opened the bedroom door. Both stopped abruptly when they saw their sister in bed.

"What dat?" Beth pointed a pudgy finger at the huge lump that was Ruth's leg.

Ruth pulled the blankets back so they could see. "Dr. Watson put this hard stuff on my leg so it won't hurt so much."

"How did you get hurted?" Timmy wanted to know.

She pondered for a moment before deciding on an explanation. "I did something Daddy told me not to do."

"You were dis'bedient?" His tongue had difficulty forming the word often used by their parents before a spanking. His wide eyes expressed disbelief that his big sister could have done such a thing.

"Yes, I was."

"Me kiss it better," Beth offered, lifting a short leg to clamber onto the bed.

Grandma grabbed her quickly. "Let me hold you and you kiss Ruthie that way. It will hurt her if you make her bed wiggle."

Beth accepted the explanation, planting a wet kiss on Ruth's cheek. "All better," she pronounced, then wiggled out of Grandma's arms. "Go play now." Timmy followed enthusiastically.

Grandma chuckled. "I think your cast impressed him

more than his most recent spanking. Are you still up to getting your hair washed?"

"Yes, please." She felt grimy and rumpled.

By the time Grandma had shampooed her hair, administered the sponge bath, and helped her into a clean nightgown, Ruth felt more than ready to relax against the pillows. This gave her a clear view of her cast, which extended from the middle of her foot to her upper leg, propped on several folded blankets. Her curiosity rippled to life. Too bad Theo wasn't here to explain. He'd told her about the various bones in her leg, and he would probably know which one she had broken. He would also ramble on at length about the substance from which her cast was made, who discovered its use in helping broken limbs mend properly, and what had been used before. They had often laughed together about how much they enjoyed discovering facts other people found boring or useless.

Shifting her gaze to the sunny day beyond her window, she wished he were still only a mile and a half away. He'd know how to help her make sense of her tangled thoughts and how to help her escape the horrible feeling of guilt over Sunset. Not only had she failed her horse, she'd let her parents down. They had worked hard and saved carefully to be able to buy him. Ever-present tears overflowed.

"You're looking better." Dr. Watson's cheery voice roused her. "How do you feel?"

She swiped at her cheeks, hoping he hadn't noticed. "Not bad, all things considering."

He leaned over her head, probing around the large lump over her left ear. "Does your head hurt much?"

"Not a lot unless I move it quickly."

"Do you remember tripping over the water bucket at

school?"

Puzzled, she corrected him, struggling to keep her voice steady. "I didn't get hurt at school. This happened when my horse fell."

His eyes twinkled as he backed away from her. "I just wanted to see how much you remembered. How many brothers do you have?"

"Three."

"Sisters?"

"One."

He pulled the covers away from her leg. "Let's look at this. Hmmm." She tried not to wince as he ran a finger around the inside of both ends of the cast. "The swelling seems to be going down well. I'd like you to stay put for the weekend. Monday we'll look at replacing the cast, since this one's getting too big. Once we have your leg stabilized, you can start getting around. I'll bring a pair of crutches next week."

"How soon can I go back to school?"

"I'd like you to wait at least another week." He looked at her soberly. "Your fall gave you a serious concussion and we have no way of knowing when your head has fully recovered. Even after you're out of bed, you'll tire easily. You'll be much better off at home where you can rest whenever you need to."

When she tried to suggest otherwise to her parents that evening, they supported Dr. Watson. "There's no need for you to push yourself," Mom said firmly. "There's only one week of school left, and we're spending most of the time practicing for the concert anyway."

"What about you having to push yourself? You haven't been feeling well, either."

"I'm not sick. I'm just expecting a baby. Being in a classroom again is great fun." Mom's sparkling eyes verified her words.

"But it's my last chance!" Ruth wailed, feeling the aggravating tears pushing through again.

"Last chance for what, honey?" Mom asked.

Ruth sniffed, trying to form a coherent reply. "I don't know. I just want to be there for the last day."

"I think I understand." Mom smoothed Ruth's hair away from her face. "It's hard to know your final day as a teacher passed without your being aware, isn't it?"

As usual, Mom's perception defined Ruth's feelings precisely. She nodded, not trusting herself to speak.

Dad knelt beside her bed. "Ruth, I know how important this feels to you, because your health feels the same to me. All I want is for you to recover completely. We'll make sure you get to the school for the concert, but I can't help you disregard Dr. Watson's instructions."

Only the love in his voice silenced her protests. Missing this last week with her students would be one more entry on the list of negatives resulting from her own poor choices.

fourteen

Saturday dragged by. With Mom home, Grandma Lucy had gone back into town to give Mrs. Spencer a break. Ruth could hear Timmy and Beth chattering while Mom did household chores. She watched Dad and the boys working around the farmyard. Every once in a while, one of them would look toward her window and wave. During meals, the sounds of her family's conversation drifted to her room. A feeling of helpless isolation threatened to overwhelm her. Looking around her room for something to distract her thoughts, she noticed her Bible on her dressing table where she'd put it while unpacking from her stay at the Pierces'. How long had it been since she'd opened it for personal reading? *Months. Maybe even over a year.* She easily recalled the anticipation with which she'd read as a young girl. Some days it had felt like a particular Scripture passage had been written just for her. Would it happen again?

Unfortunately, the table sat in the opposite corner from her bed. She moved her good leg to the edge of the bed, then tried to get her cast to follow. It wouldn't budge. She pushed the covers to the side near the wall, grasped the white mountain with both hands, and placed it as close to the edge of the bed as possible. She lay back against the pillows at an awkward angle, breathless from effort. Her strength seemed to have drained to nothing. After several moments' rest, she tried again. Bracing her good foot on the floor, she lifted the heavy leg. Too late, she realized how precarious her seating had become. She toppled helplessly off the side.

Mom came in a rush. "Ruth! Are you all right?"

Both her head and her leg had begun throbbing again. Her pride also stung, not helped by the tears she couldn't hide. "I just wanted my Bible," she whimpered.

"Why didn't you ask?" Mom helped her to a sitting position on the floor, then braced her so she could lift herself back onto the bed. The extra pair of hands made maneuvering the cast much easier. Mom plumped the pillows behind Ruth's shoulders, smoothed the covers, and placed the Bible on the edge of the bed. "I wish you would have called."

"I didn't want to bother you."

"Helping you get well is not a bother." Mom kissed her forehead. "You must be getting pretty bored. Shall I send the little ones in to entertain you?"

"I'd like to see them, but my head is pounding again," she admitted sheepishly.

"Sleep is probably the best thing for you. Next time, call me, please?" Mom shut the door softly behind her.

Ruth slept restlessly. Theo's face drifted in and out of her dreams. When she called out to him, he disappeared. She awoke with wet cheeks. While she regretted hurting Jed's feelings, Theo's withdrawal had created the deepest wound. She wanted desperately to restore contact, but that would only postpone the pain. Sooner or later, he would fall in love with the nurse who could enhance his practice. Ruth wished she had decided to learn nursing. Dad's arrival with the checkerboard made a welcome distraction.

The next morning, Grandma Lucy showed up while the

rest of the family was eating breakfast. "I've come to keep you company while everyone's gone," she announced to Ruth. "How are you feeling?" Her piercing gaze defied the younger woman to be less than honest.

Ruth didn't even try to fool her. "Frustrated and confused."

Grandma smiled understandingly. "You mean you're arguing with your Heavenly Father again?"

Denial rose and dissipated quickly. "I guess you're right. You did tell me this would be a perfect place to learn trust."

Grandma pulled the rocking chair close to Ruth's side. "What's the trouble?"

"I feel like I've wrecked everything and have no way of putting it back together." Grandma's silence encouraged her to continue. "Jed told me if he didn't hear from me by today, he'd make the announcement cancelling our wedding. Mr. Albertson has already bought windows for us, and Millers have hauled a load of lumber out to Harpers' for the new cabin. I've made life pretty embarrassing for Jed."

Grandma didn't contradict her. "He'll survive."

"But I feel so badly."

"You'd feel worse if you'd gone through with it. Will you choose to trust his Heavenly Father to take care of him?"

She weighed the question, pondering its significance. "It seems unfair to expect God to make up for my mistakes."

"The Bible is full of illustrations of God doing just that. Jesus' death on the cross was nothing more or less than God's ultimate atonement for mankind's biggest mistake."

"I'd never thought about it that way."

Grandma's gaze never left Ruth's face. "You're not alone.

It's easy to think we have to fix or hide our failures rather than coming to our Father just as we are."

"I feel like I've failed my school children, too. If I hadn't gotten so messed up over Jed and Theo, I'd be able to finish the school year with them."

Grandma stopped rocking. "Theo?"

Ruth's face warmed. Mentioning him had been a slip of the tongue she'd immediately hoped Grandma would miss. Hesitantly, she told about the letter and her feelings since. "I miss him so badly it hurts."

"May I ask an impertinent question?" She waited for Ruth's nod. "What would you say if he asked you to marry him?"

Shock numbed Ruth all over. She finally managed a protest. "We're just best friends!"

"There's no better way to start a terrific marriage," Grandma declared firmly.

Ruth refused to let her mind dwell on the possibility. "I wouldn't be the kind of wife he needs."

Humorous twinkles appeared in Grandma's blue eyes. "Wouldn't it be better to let God decide that one?"

"It always comes back to trust, doesn't it?"

"Now you're catching on. Shall we pray about all this together?" She clasped Ruth's hands. "You start and I'll finish."

At first Ruth didn't know what to say. Other than her desperate appeal while riding Sunset, her prayers had been as nonexistent as her Bible reading. She began hesitantly. "Heavenly Father, I'm sorry I've been so stubborn. Because I refused to trust You, I've affected a lot of people." With the admission, her thoughts seemed to flow much easier. "I'm asking you to make up to Jed for the hurt I've caused him. Please help me continue to trust You with my future, and bless my students even though I can't be with them on this last week of school. Give Mom strength as she takes my place. I ask for patience for myself, and for Your help in learning whatever You want to teach me." Her voice dropped to a whisper. "Please bless Theo, Lord."

Grandma's voice took over comfortingly. "Father, I ask for Your comfort for Ruth. While I know You don't always show us Your working in others' lives, would you please let her see what You're doing for Jed while he adjusts to their decision not to marry. I also sense You're not finished with her and Theo, despite the way circumstances look now. Please bring peace and healing to Ruth's heart and give her an assurance of Your will. Thank you for Ruth. She's brought much joy to many of our lives and we look forward to seeing the joy You bring to hers. Amen."

They sat hand in hand in comforting silence until Ruth ventured, "I wish trust were as easy to learn as the multiplication tables."

Grandma smiled. "It's harder because your emotions fight so hard against it. But in some ways it is just as easy. The only way you learned your multiplication tables was by practice. I'm still having to practice trust, to choose between trying to figure things out myself or waiting to see what God does."

"It's hard to remember to choose."

"Have you read the book of Job since we talked about it? Chapters 38 through 41 present an awesome picture of God as He describes Himself. You should read them sometime, along with Psalm 139. The struggle isn't nearly so hard when you begin to get a glimpse of Who it is you're trusting."

"I was going to do some Bible reading yesterday, but got sidetracked." Ruth giggled as she told of her mishap.

"You wonderful, stubbornly independent woman!" Grandma exclaimed through laughter. "I don't suppose you thought of how badly you could injure yourself."

"Not until I was on the floor in a painful heap."

"You won't try getting out of bed on your own again until Dr. Watson gives you leave, right?"

Ruth shook her head. "Though it is frustrating to have to call for somebody for something as simple as using the chamberpot."

"I know." Grandma patted her hand comfortingly. "I spent several months in a hospital in England before I met Mr. Barry. Humility is no easier to learn than trust." She picked up Ruth's Bible from where it lay on the floor beside the bed. "May I read aloud to you?"

"Sure." Ruth snuggled into her covers, prepared for a treat. As she expected, Grandma turned to the chapters to which she'd referred earlier. With each thunderous question from the Almighty, Ruth felt her own foolishness at demanding an explanation for anything. Then with barely a pause, Grandma swished a few pages and continued reading. "O Lord, thou hast searched me, and known me. Thou knowest my downsitting and mine uprising, thou understandest my thought afar off. . . How precious also are thy thoughts unto me, O God! how great is the sum of them!" The words wrapped Ruth in a comforting cocoon. The fog of confusion lifted, and all at once she understood what Grandma had repeatedly tried to tell her. God didn't choose to withhold explanations about His ways just to be difficult. His plan was simply too overwhelming for her to comprehend. Rather than offering a defense of His ways,

He extended the assurance of His unfaltering love, His continuing presence with her through both easy times and hard.

Her eyes slid shut as she continued to explore these unfamiliar ideas. Because of what God said about Himself, trust was more than hoping for an invisible safety net. It represented her confidence in God's faithfulness to His own character. The fear she'd carried for seven years retreated as she realized she no longer had to be afraid of loss. Heartbreak wouldn't come her way again unless by Divine plan. Though she still couldn't comprehend why He might permit such pain, He'd help her endure it. A delicious sense of freedom made her tingle all over.

She opened her eyes to see Grandma watching her with a loving smile. "It finally makes sense," she whispered.

Grandma's grin widened. "I wish you could see your own face. You look like you just discovered gold."

"I wish I could feel this way forever."

"You won't, though," Grandma stated matter-of-factly. "That's why you have to rely on what you know, not what you feel."

"How do you do it?" Ruth wished for an easy formula.

"I never let myself forget what God says about Himself. Since He cannot lie, His words form an indestructible foundation for our faith. Sometimes I remember easily. Other times it's a struggle. I have to get alone and read passages like Psalm 139 aloud. I've never been sorry for choosing to trust Him, even when it's hard." Pounding on the front door broke the contemplative silence. Grandma hustled off to respond.

Ruth glanced out the window to see if she could figure out who'd come, then looked again. A black stallion stood tied to the corral fence. Before she had time to panic, Jed appeared in the doorway, turning his hat around and around in his hands. "May I come in?"

"Sure." Ruth gestured toward the rocking chair, wondering why Grandma hadn't followed him.

"I was real sorry to hear about your accident." He finally quit worrying the hat and set it on his knees. His fingers drummed on the arms of the chair.

"It was my own stupidity," Ruth assured him, inwardly wondering where the oppressive sense of guilt had gone. She felt no less responsible for what had happened, just ready to leave it in the past.

"It was partly my fault." Jed's words came out quickly before she could interrupt. "You were right about us not being suited. I can't explain why. This morning I just realized we'll be better off as friends. I told folks this morning that the weddin's off. Mr. Miller and Mr. Albertson both told me to keep the buildin' supplies, anyway. I wanted you to know I'm not upset, and your dad said I could come see you before they got home."

"Thank you." The words barely fit past the lump in her throat. "I'm sorry I didn't say no when you first asked."

"I prob'ly wasn't too smart for askin', but mistakes is part of livin'. I hope you won't mind if I come around once in a while."

His poor grammar made her feel like a cat who'd been rubbed the wrong way, but she focussed on the meaning behind it. "You'll always be welcome. When you discover the right girl, I hope you let me meet her."

"Sure." The familiar pink tinged his ears. "I best be goin'. Thanks for seein' me."

Grandma reappeared with a lunch tray shortly after Ruth

heard the front door close behind Jed. "I hope you're hungry."

Ruth pretended to glare at her. "What if I had needed moral support?"

Grandma snorted. "The poor boy was so nervous he could hardly walk straight. If anything, *he* needed the moral support."

Ruth accepted a jelly sandwich and briefly related their conversation. "I would have expected him to never speak to me again."

"Jed's made of finer stuff than that," Grandma Lucy contradicted. "Besides, didn't I tell you God would straighten things out?"

Ruth just grinned, silently hoping He'd work as quickly to make sense of her relationship with Theo.

fifteen

Dr. Watson waited until Wednesday to release Ruth from bed rest. Grandma Lucy continued her daily trips from town to keep the McEvan household running smoothly.

As promised, Dad made sure Ruth was able to attend the end-of-the-year concert. She'd never felt more proud of her students. The entire program flowed smoothly, showing the hours of practice they'd invested. No church choir could have produced better music than Julie and Karin's duet.

After a month, Dr. Watson finally consented to remove the cast. Ruth spent the next week exercising her leg as much as she could tolerate. At long last, she managed the short distance between the farm and school. She'd asked Mom to let her do the final cleaning and clearing up. It was something she simply had to do alone. She pushed open the door, noticing the large pot of steaming water on the warm stove. Dad must have come by earlier to build a fire and put the water on to heat. This last month would have been unbearable without his and Mom's continuous loving gestures.

Seeing the empty desks brought back her last afternoon as teacher, when she'd sat at the front of the room crying as she read Theo's farewell letter. She'd made the right decision, she reminded herself firmly. The pain of separation would come eventually. Better to face it now than later.

One by one, she washed the desks carefully. The town

162

school board had offered to buy them, along with anything else this building no longer needed. Each swipe of her cloth brought back a different memory—each youngster she'd taught, their strengths and weaknesses, charms and moods. Julie's desk had been emptied; she'd obviously even washed it out before leaving. Phillip's, right behind, remained stuffed with scraps of paper as well as a collection of leaves, sticks, rocks, and other items Ruth didn't want to identify. By the time she reached the back row of desks, her thoughts had drifted even further to her own years as a student. She'd used this desk, with Theo right behind her.

They had shared only one year of formal schooling before he had left for the city, but on that first day he had waited for her to choose a seat, then selected the one directly behind her. She wiped the wood caressingly. It had taken wrong and foolish decisions to make her aware of the love that had grown between them. Even her dislike for the city wouldn't hold her back if he asked her to marry him.

But it wouldn't happen, she knew. He still thought she wanted to marry Jed. If he had acquired the position in the hospital of his choice, he wouldn't be able to come home until Christmas at least. Maybe things would change then, though she wouldn't build her hopes on it. If nothing else, the past weeks had taught her to entrust each of her moments to her Heavenly Father. Her recovery time had given her hours on her own to read Scripture. She still found some passages dry, but others seemed written just for her— like the one she'd found in Isaiah. ". . .in quietness and in confidence shall be your strength."

She found herself humming snatches of hymns as she continued her farewell to her precious classroom. Misplaced mittens and lost pencils showed up in the strangest places, like behind the bookshelf from which she removed used textbooks to add to the rapidly filling crates. Her damp cloth removed pencil marks and sticky spots. Her leg was throbbing by the time she'd completed everything she wanted to do. Even the large teacher's desk at the front had been emptied and cleaned in every corner of every drawer. She dipped and wrung her rag one more time and hobbled to the chalkboard. If her leg would hold her up for just a couple more minutes, everything would be spotless. She reached for the highest corner, trying to keep most of her weight on her right leg. Overbalancing, she would have fallen had not a pair of masculine arms grabbed her from behind.

"I don't think your doctor would approve of this activity," his familiar voice chided.

Shock immobilized her for a moment before she turned in his arms to hug him ecstatically. "Theo! Where did you come from?"

His beloved chuckle rumbled beside her ear. "Where do you think? Come, I can tell it's long past time for you to sit down." He guided her gently to her chair and hoisted himself onto her desk. Without removing his gaze from her face, he remarked, "You could have really hurt yourself again, you know."

Was the warmth in his brown eyes for real or just the product of her hopeful imagination? Since she'd seen him two years ago, he'd grown a beard, which most attractively added a few years to his appearance. He looked more filled out than she remembered. The boy she recalled had unquestionably become a full-grown man. "I'd like to know how you happened to be right behind me at that precise moment. I didn't even hear you come in."

"I meant to sneak up on you." That wonderful smile parted his beard. "Your humming made it easier than I expected."

Her cheeks warmed. "I hadn't counted on anyone being close enough to hear it."

"I'm glad I did. You sounded and look happy."

"I am." The words sounded far too simple for the contentment she'd found in the past couple of weeks.

"I can tell. You look like it goes all the way through, too." His gaze searched hers with comforting intensity. "You're not fighting your Heavenly Father any more."

Her smile felt like it came from the deepest part of her heart. "I finally realized it's stupid to resist Him when He loves me so much. But I can't believe you're actually here. From your last letter, I figured it would be months, if not years, before you made it back. Did you get your job in the city?"

"No." The single word came out tersely. His gaze travelled slowly over her face, then returned to her eyes. "I decided I didn't want it after all. But if you don't mind, I'd rather talk about you. Mom said you'd broken your leg and given yourself a concussion. What happened?"

She wondered how much to tell him, since much of the story involved her feelings for him. A pang of regret knifed through her. Not so long ago, she wouldn't have even considered weighing her words.

"Hey, this is Theo," he reminded, leaning down to clasp one of her hands. "Good old Theo. You can tell me anything."

Rather than pulling away, she wanted to snuggle back into his arms. She began talking to keep herself from act-

ing on the impulse. "Everything happened that day. Dad
brought your letter by here on his way home, and pointed
out I probably shouldn't be writing to you anymore. Your
letter told me the same thing." Theo's grip tightened com-
passionately, but he didn't interrupt. "I couldn't stand the
thought of losing my best friend simply because I'd agreed
to marry Jed. Then Jed invited me to go riding with him
later that evening, and we had words."

"Because of my letter?" he asked with regret in his eyes.

"No. I don't think he was ever aware of our correspondence. It actually started because Sunset outran his black
stallion. I'd never let it happen before, but that evening I
was too upset to pay attention. Our conversation, or argu-
ment, or whatever you want to call it, gradually included
everything from his mother to my teaching. By the time he
suggested I might not want to marry him, I agreed readily."
She smiled up at her friend. It felt so good to be confiding
in him once again. "He's a really nice fellow and will make
some woman a terrific husband. Just not me. He needs
someone who finds the farm as all-absorbing as he does."

"And someone who won't disagree with him much," Theo
supplied with a twinkle.

She giggled. "That, too. He's so goodhearted, though, I
still sometimes feel like a wretch for breaking our engagement."

"Don't." A mysterious light in his eyes accompanied his
whispered advice.

"I keep telling myself the same thing. Anyway, he offered to escort me home, but I told him not to bother. I
have no idea how far Sunset and I rode that evening, but
when I finally stopped crying enough to realize where we
were, we'd reached your dad's east pasture. I put Sunset

into a gallop, he stumbled and fell, and next thing I knew, I was in bed with a sore head and a huge leg."

"I'm sorry." His quiet sympathy wrapped around her heart.

"Me too. There's so much I wish I could go back and undo."

"Like what?"

"Like deciding I wouldn't depend on God for anything because He wouldn't tell me why He hadn't made things happen differently at the river. If I'd been trusting Him all along, I wouldn't have panicked when they told me the school was closing, and I'd have told Jed no the night he proposed."

"You're sure about that?"

"About Jed?"

He nodded.

"Absolutely. I wish I didn't have to be totally dependent on my parents, but I'm willing to wait and let God work that out."

A delighted smile lit his face. "You've come a long way since your last letter."

"You're probably wondering why I didn't write to you again."

"Not really. If I can still read you as well as I used to, the potential change in our friendship shook you up as badly as it did me." He still retained his hold on her hand. "Remember what I wrote about something changing my mind about setting up a practice here?" She nodded, unable to tear her gaze from those wonderfully soft, dark eyes. His voice dropped to a ragged whisper. "That something was you and Jed."

Hope silently overflowed inside her, though she tried to

still her racing heart. His doctor's fingers would detect it in a second.

Though his thumb rubbed her wrist ever so gently, he made no comment about her pulse. "I've known since we were both still in school you were the one I wanted to marry. I didn't say anything before I left for fear of scaring you off. Did I do you wrong?"

She shook her head, while trying to absorb both his words and the overwhelming affection in his gaze. Even a month ago, she would have been so intimidated by this much caring she would have pushed it away.

The worry wrinkle disappeared from between his eyes. "I've been hoping and praying I did the right thing. When you wrote to me about accepting Jed's proposal, I realized I'd waited too long. Distance didn't give me an option other than praying something would happen to change your mind." His eyes offered her the same heartfelt devotion Dad's showed when he looked at Mom, and young Lionel's held for Sara.

Strangely, rather than being frightened of the intensity, she felt like her heart had finally come home. She spoke the first coherent words that came to mind. "I thought you'd marry a nurse."

His laughter eased some of the tension hovering between them. "Several of them tried so hard, it was embarrassing. None of them came even close to replacing my best friend." He walked around to the front of her desk and paced back and forth. "I couldn't believe it when Mom wrote that you and Jed had called the wedding off. When I read you'd been hurt, it was all I could do to finish out my contract at the hospital. I wanted desperately to rush home and take care of you myself."

"I wished for you," she assured him. "Dr. Watson did as much as he could for my leg and my head, but he couldn't make my heartache go away."

He finally quit pacing. "Because of my letter?"

"Sort of. Even if we did start writing again, I figured I'd have to give you up again when you found the girl you wanted to marry."

"Dear little friend." He pulled her from the chair into a wonderfully possessive embrace. "The girl I want is right here. Will you please marry me?"

"Yes," she whispered against his shoulder.

"Did you just say what I thought you said?"

She leaned back to smile into his eyes. "Yes."

Joy filled his eyes as he leaned down to kiss her tentatively. When he lifted his head, she reached up a hand to pull him down for a second, more thorough kiss. He looked as dazed as she felt when they finally looked at each other again. "You'd better be Mrs. Theodore Pierce the next time you do that," he warned shakily, "because I'm not sure I'll behave responsibly. Come. I want to show you something." When they reached the doorway, he stood behind her, arms around her waist. "What do you see?"

His horse, Shadow, grazed near the edge of the bush beside a delicate-looking bay filly. White patches above each of the filly's hooves looked like socks, contrasting with her dark mane and tail. No horse could have looked more different from Sunset yet just as striking. "She's beautiful," Ruth breathed.

"I had a bit of money saved up. When I heard about Sunset, I thought this filly would make a good bribe in case you weren't sure about marrying me."

She turned to look into his eyes. "Is she really mine?"

"Only if you marry me."

She brushed her fingers down his beard. "I've missed your weird sense of humor."

"Who's laughing? You'd better marry me after that little display back there by the desk."

"Who started it?"

He grinned, tightening his arms around her. "I've missed you, too." His expression sobered. "I came so close to losing you. Is it my imagination or did you really say you wanted to marry this small town doctor?"

For answer, she laid her head against his chest in another hug. As a boy this person had proved his friendship. As a man he offered his love. Nothing she'd imagined or hoped for had come close to the fulfillment of committing herself to him for always. In trusting her Heavenly Father's direction of her steps, she'd found her heart's desire.

A Letter To Our Readers

Dear Reader:

In order that we might better contribute to your reading enjoyment, we would appreciate your taking a few minutes to respond to the following questions. When completed, please return to the following:

Rebecca Germany, Editor
Heartsong Presents
P.O. Box 719
Uhrichsville, Ohio 44683

1. Did you enjoy reading *Beckoning Streams*?
   ❏ Very much. I would like to see more books
      by this author!
   ❏ Moderately
      I would have enjoyed it more if _____

   _____

2. Are you a member of *Heartsong Presents*? Yes   No
   If no, where did you purchase this book? _____

   _____

3. What influenced your decision to purchase this
   book? (Check those that apply.)

   ❏ Cover   ❏ Back cover copy

   ❏ Title   ❏ Friends

   ❏ Publicity   ❏ Other _____

4. On a scale from 1 (poor) to 10 (superior), please rate the following elements.

___Heroine ___Plot

___Hero ___Inspirational theme

___Setting ___Secondary characters

5. What settings would you like to see covered in *Heartsong Presents* books?

_____

_____

6. What are some inspirational themes you would like to see treated in future books?_____

_____

_____

7. Would you be interested in reading other *Heartsong Presents* titles? ❏ Yes ❏ No

8. Please check your age range:
❏ Under 18 ❏ 18-24 ❏ 25-34
❏ 35-45 ❏ 46-55 ❏ Over 55

9. How many hours per week do you read? —————

Name _____

Occupation _____

Address _____

City _____ State _____ Zip _____

Heartsong Presents

Settings Around the Globe!

__*Candleshine* by Colleen L. Reece—With the onslaught of World War II, Candleshine Thatcher dedicates her life to nursing, and then her heart to a brave Marine lieutenant. Theirs was a wartime romance, a wisp of a breeze in the sultry South Pacific, a promise made amid threats of invasion and attack. HP07

__*Drums of Shelomoh* by Yvonne Lehman—As a nurse, Crystal Janis has seen it all. That is, until her visit to a mission outpost in Rhodesia, Africa. A much-needed vacation becomes a series of challenging crises and a chance for lasting love. HP37

__*Search for Tomorrow* by Mary Hawkins—Broken in body and in spirit but hoping nonetheless for a new beginning, Abigail Brandon accepts a job as a housekeeper for the Stevens family on their farm outside Brisbane, Australia. HP42

__*River of Peace* by Janelle Burnham—The year is 1930. Ida Thomas has taken the job of schoolteacher in the remote village of Dawson Creek, British Columbia. Will she find a man she can truly love and know peace like a river? HP100

···· Hearts ♥ng ····

········· Presents ·········

Great Inspirational Romance at a Great Price!

Heartsong Presents books are inspirational romances in contemporary and historical settings, designed to give you an enjoyable, spirit-lifting reading experience. You can choose from 120 wonderfully written titles from some of today's best authors like Colleen L. Reece, Brenda Bancroft, Janelle Jamison, and many others.

When ordering quantities less than twelve, above titles are $2.95 each.

Heartsong Presents
Love Stories Are Rated G!

That's for godly, gratifying, and of course, great! If you love a thrilling love story, but don't appreciate the sordidness of popular paperback romances, **Heartsong Presents** is for you. In fact, **Heartsong Presents** is the *only inspirational romance book club*, the only one featuring love stories where Christian faith is the primary ingredient in a marriage relationship.

Sign up today to receive your first set of four, never before published Christian romances. Send no money now; you will receive a bill with the first shipment. You may cancel at any time without obligation, and if you aren't completely satisfied with any selection, you may return the books for an immediate refund!

Imagine. . .four new romances every month—two historical, two contemporary—with men and women like you who long to meet the one God has chosen as the love of their lives. . .all for the low price of $9.97 postpaid.

To join, simply complete the coupon below and mail to the address provided. **Heartsong Presents** romances are rated G for another reason: They'll arrive *Godspeed!*